MY FAVORITE HOBO

Written by

COLENE COPELAND

FOLLOW YOUR DREAMS

Colene Copeland

D1490486

MY FAVORITE HOBO

Manufactured in the U.S.A.

Library of Congress Catalog Card number: 2001117684

ISBN: 0-939810-25-5

First Edition

b.

DEDICATION

To my husband, Robert.
To my best friend
and favorite hobo, Robert.
Our forty-four years together
were the best years of my life.

MY THANKS

To the hobos who enriched our lives in so many ways.

To the Ellison kids: Iva (Case), Laura (Harmon), Bill and Ernie Ellison, friends forever.

To Beverly Forson, an excellent pickle maker and winner of awards for growing king size apples--who helped me remember the spices that Mama put in her pickles.

To Shirley Pershawn who aided with the research of events through the years.

Last but not least, to my granddaughter, Christina Bolter, a language teacher in the Universtiy of Hawaii, for her expertise in editing. Christina was also a published author at age 14 with her "Apples In The Sky."

c.

CONTENTS

d.

February 2001 - Looking Back

Growing up as I did after the depression on a dairy farm in Missouri, I remember the hobos off the freight trains who ate at our table. Our family never refused food to any one of them.

The days of hobos are gone forever. Today the homeless are called street people. Times have changed, but hunger is still with us.

Someone very dear to me was once homeless. Because of him and the hungry souls who beat a path to our door, I remain sympathetic to their suffering.

On a cold, clear day--a miserable one for street people--I spotted one such fellow standing on the dismal gray sidewalk, clutching a small, brown paper bag to his chest. Clearly, the contents of that bag were important to him. A sandwich, perhaps. I knew sandwiches were passed out often to the hungry.

One of the man's pant legs was torn, exposing his body from his ankle to his waist. His soiled pocket hung inside out. He wore no cap and his jacket was dirty and extremely ragged.

The poor man stood there in front of the busy downtown mall as noonday traffic sped by. Was he ill?--mentally unsound?--a wino? Was there anyone who cared, I wondered?

My home was only a few blocks away. Perhaps if I hurried, I could help him. In a few minutes, I was searching through some men's clothing in the spare closet. I came up with a warm, bulky jacket, a pair of pants, and two flannel shirts that looked like they would fit. Adding to that some socks and a pair of woolen gloves, I quickly headed back.

Returning to the place where he'd been, I found the ragged man had not moved far. I pulled over to the curb, quickly got out, and handed him the bag of clothing except for the jacket, which I hung over his arm.

"You look like you could use these things," I said, as I got back into my car.

His face showed no expression. As I pulled away, he gave me a slight nod of his head.

Curiosity overtook me. I drove around the block to have a look. Already he had on the new jacket and it seemed to fit O.K. The soiled one lie at his feet. The next time I circled the block, he was walking hurriedly down the street to an area behind Cavenger's Diner where there were public restrooms used solely by the street people. On my next time around, he had reached his destination and was standing by a battered telephone booth. He stood there for a few moments looking into the bag I'd given him before disappearing into one of the buildings. I parked so I could snoop a little longer.

Suddenly, he rushed back toward the telephone booth, as if he were looking for something. The brown paper bag he'd held before was on the sidewalk. Finding it empty, he placed an open hand across his mouth in disbelief. Looking around on the ground, he located what appeared to be a small bundle of letters, tied with a string. Ever so gently, he picked them up and pressed them to his chest. After returning the letters to the bag, he slid them into the big pocket of the new coat he now wore and tapped the pocket as if to say, "safe again." Having done that, he placed his hands together prayerfully, looked toward the heavens and nodded.

What had been in those letters? They were, I assumed, his only possessions and so precious to him. I would never know for sure.

Driving home, I felt sad and depressed. I was glad to have helped a little, but it was so little.

That evening, as I sat in front of my nice, warm fireplace, in my nice, warm house, I thought of the less fortunate. My eyes drifted to a picture on the mantel of me and my best friend when we were kids. I sat and gazed into the fire, remembering how a homeless man had shared with him: another story waiting to be told.

This story began when I was nine years old. It's about a lonely little girl and her struggles throughout her childhood. And it's about hobos, hard times, and handouts. It's also about dreams and determination.

Let me share it with you.

Chapter 1.

MAY 1939 - AGE 9

"Better get off the railroad tracks," Billy shouted. "If ol' lady Garst sees you, you'll be in big trouble!"

Billy was right about our neighbor, but, ask me if I cared. I wanted to see if any hobos were getting off the afternoon freight train.

Not many folks in Watson were as friendly with the bo's (short for hobos) as my family. At every turn I was warned. "Better be careful of those guys," they'd say. How would they know? The hobos were simply poor men who rode the freights from town to town and job to job. They rode in box cars, on the flat beds, up on the fuel tankers, and inside of hoppers. They took any way available to get them to food and work. It was their way of dealing with hard times. At first they carried a hoe, giving them the appearance of being ready for work. They were called Hoe-Boys. Later this nickname became "hobos."

There were the bums who were dirty and different. They, too, rode the freights and asked for food. But never for work.

Sometimes the hobos were invited into our house to eat. Especially the ones we knew. And sometimes Daddy let them sleep on the hay in the barn, but never the bums.

When a bum knocked on our door, Mama quickly hooked the screen. She'd make him a sandwich and a drink and invite him to eat on the back porch. My family never turned anyone away hungry.

I wasn't afraid of the bo's. However, there *was* a strangeness about nearly all of them--something sort of mystic. Maybe it was the way they lived. I hoped, but never knew for sure, if they could be trusted. When they told us their name, were they telling the truth?

All of them had nicknames like Minnesota Millie, Nashville Ned, Steamtrain Wally or River Johnny. I never told anybody, not even Iva and Laura, who were my best friends and Billy's older sisters, but sometimes, when Daddy wasn't around, I felt uneasy with some of them. Looking back, I know now, I should have told my parents.

My family moved to Watson in 1937, when I was seven. Our house was the first house outside the city limits. The railroad went right through our 400 acres. In the two years we'd lived there we had become well-acquainted with quite a few hobos. Daddy was known to them as a man who always had plenty of work waiting when they showed up. We ran a dairy. Besides that, they all knew about my mother's good cooking. Word got around. The men headed straight for our place, knowing they would not leave hungry.

I knew the hobos had their own set of markings to let each other know about where to get a meal, medical attention, and other help they might require. We knew our place was marked. Mom and Daddy said they didn't mind being known as folks who fed the hungry.

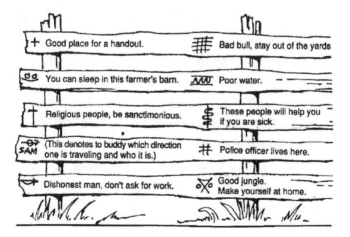

One afternoon, at about two o'clock, I'd heard the freight slowing long before it rumbled in to Watson. Miss Nuckols caught me staring out the window, not paying any attention. She was giving us our weekly spelling test and wasn't too happy when she had to repeat the last two words for me. Thank goodness summer vacation was only two weeks away!

The sounds of the trains set me to day-dreaming about far away places.

"Colene," she said sharply, "that freight will not help you with those spelling words." Miss Nuckols knew all my bad habits. At least she thought she did.

A lot of us kids had to cross the railroad tracks to get home after school. Sometimes we had to wait quite a while for the train to pull up. But today, the freight cars had been uncoupled so that automobiles and those of us on foot could cross the tracks.

In any twenty-four hour period, ten to twelve trains passed through or stopped in our little town. Like best friends, I never grew tired of them. Not the loud ones switching around in town, nor the distant ones coming and going, nor the five or six which carried passengers. I loved the sound of the metal wheels on the railroad tracks, and I *loved* the passengers. Many of them waved and smiled as they traveled through Watson.

Looking back on it all now, I think I must have looked strange to the city folks passing through. I was a tanned little country girl in overalls, my long brown hair tied with bright ribbons. I'd climb to the top of our big gate by the tracks, waving for as long as anyone was in sight. Greeting the trains brought a bit of joy to my lonely life.

I came to know the faces of all the engineers on all the trains as well as the brakemen and other regular workers. Even the waiters in the dining cars watched for me and smiled and waved. I was never disappointed.

There was a black man who worked in the dining car on the 10 A.M. and 6 P.M. passenger trains who always waved. One day, he bent down to wave to me out of the window. He was waving and smiling. I loved his friendly smile. Suddenly, the tray of food he was carrying went sliding off his hand. I felt so guilty. I wondered if he had gotten fired. The next time I saw him, I waved and waved. He was still smiling.

The engine had sidetracked several box cars to the grain elevator, where workers were loading up corn and wheat. From where I was standing, it appeared to be a 4-6-2 Pacific. The numbers had to do with the wheels on the engine. This one was pulling about seventy or eighty cars.

The hobos could figure out just how long they could be off the freight in order to catch it when it left town. Sometimes, when they found work and food, they'd catch the next freight. There was always another one to catch.

There I stood on the railroad tracks by a stopped train, looking for hobos. The neighbor could gawk at me all she pleased. I'd go when I'd seen what I wanted to see.

It was worth the wait. I spied them coming, way down near the caboose. It was Stovepipe for sure--he had a wooden leg and I knew his walk and his clothes. With him was probably Nashville Ned. The two men moved slowly toward town. Why had they waited until now to walk in? The train had been stopped for at least an hour.

Their slow, metered pace was eerie. It was unusually hot for May. Heat vapors from the blistering railroad cinders boiled up around them in a ghostly fashion.

Out of the corner of my eye, I saw Mrs. Garst rubbernecking at me. One hand was rammed down in her soiled apron pocket and the other was cupped over her eyes, blocking out the sun. I do believe her favorite thing to do was spy on us kids and get us into trouble with our parents.

However, she *did* have beautiful flowers in her yard and she lived for working with them. Billy's little brother, Ernie, liked to tease her. When giant peonies, in full bloom, poked through her fence, he would walk his dog up and down the sidewalk until, at last, the dog would lift his leg and wet on her flowers. Of course Mrs. Garst screamed and yelled and threatened. Ernie would take his time about walking away, laughing as he left. He knew full well his mom would switch his legs as soon as she found out.

Six-year-old Billy still watched me. He finally ran across the street to his house shouting one more warning.

"Better stop taking them ol' bums home with you. Your dad will whoop your `you-know-what.'"

"Not so, kid. They're hobos. You know the difference," I called back to him as I ran the last block home. I put up with Billy simply because his sisters were my friends.

The town's sidewalk ended at our property line. We were in the country even though it seemed like we were in town. As I stepped off the cement onto the well-worn path, the earth felt cool through the thin soles of my shoes.

My mother was the only one at home. Daddy

was in the field, planting corn. That meant I'd be doing the milking alone, again.

My older brother, Glenn, had been married about a year. My second brother, Charley, owned a couple of trucks and used them to make money hauling grain and livestock. He was never at home except to eat and get dressed up for dates. My sister, Lucille, was seventeen and a senior in high school. She would graduate in about a week. Lucille had bad asthma. She never went near the barn or the livestock without wheezing her head off. So, she helped Mom in the house. My sister Irene worked at a grocery store in Watson after school. Irene was thirteen and would graduate from the eighth grade the same night Lucille graduated from high school.

None of us kids were near each other in age. Charley was six years older than Lucille. We girls were all four years apart.

As fate would have it, I was the one left to help Daddy with the farm. It was hard work for a girl my age, but complaining was not allowed.

Even though it was 1939, we still did not have electricity. We milked at least a dozen cows by hand. The county's Rural Electrical Association, the company which put up the poles and strung the electric lines, hadn't come to us yet. Sometimes we had to do the milking by lantern light. I'd use a flashlight to find the cows, get them in, and find my way to the barn. I never told a soul, but I was scared to death of the dark.

Daddy took me to the milk barn to help when I was seven. It wasn't long before I could milk as fast as he could and became really strong. People who knew my family said I worked too hard for a little girl. Looking back at those days, I suspect that they were right. Playing with other kids was a rare treat for me.

After a snack of two hot rolls, still warm from off of the oven door, and a homemade dill pickle, I stuck my arms through the bails (handles) of four three-and-a-half-gallon, stainless steel milk pails and headed for the barn. I looked like milk buckets with legs.

The cows were at the far end of the middle pasture, about a half-mile away. If I were lucky, they would come when I called them. Most of the time they did not.

All I asked for was a single cow to hear my voice. I tilted my head back, cupped both hands around my mouth, and called as loudly as I could, "Sook cows, sook cows!" Not one of them stirred.

I asked my dad why you call a cow by saying "sook cow." His answer was that in cow language, that means "come cow." I think he must have made that up--or else he'd just bounced over too many acres of plowed ground.

What we needed was a good stock dog like our neighbors had. Their dog brought in the cows all by himself. I had begged for a puppy to train as a stock dog, but nobody had paid any attention to me. My dad brought in the cows with our pickup truck when it was dry enough, but I had to walk--sunshine, rain or snow.

Again I yelled to the cows. This time I saw some movement. It could have been one of them just switching her tail at a fly. Then Gracie, Daddy's favorite, a dependable Holstein, looked my way. She headed in. I could have kissed her! The rest would follow.

Holsteins were the dairyman's favorite. They were typically large, black and white cows, and they were gentle. Gracie was just that. She never tried to kick the milk bucket over, like some did. Her bag was always full at milking time. When she walked, milk squirted out all by itself. Four out of five of Gracie's calves had been big heifers (females). Daddy liked that. He would keep the calf until it grew up and had a baby, then he'd sell them both together and make some money. Daddy was a smart farmer.

Quickly, I hurried to the shed next to the barn

where the ground corn was kept. I filled the big metal tub with a bushel of corn. Using a one-pound coffee can, I put some in each individual grain box before the cows began filing into the milk barn. I worked fast; I didn't want to get stepped on. Once you've been stepped on by a cow, you try not to let it happen again! Thinking about it caused me to speed up.

We ground up the corn for the cows, cobbs and all, so it wasn't all that heavy.

The barn doors were open to let in some fresh air. A neighbor boy was walking home from school. He was always either whistling or walking down the middle of the road, playing his trombone. I hoped the fool wouldn't scare these four-legged beasts. All twelve of them hurried in and with them came a million flies. Each cow had a metal chain around her neck. The stalls were tied with a piece of rope and a snap. The cows knew which spot was theirs. As soon as they took their place, I snapped them in so they wouldn't move around. Grabbing the fly-sprayer, I gave them all a good shot of the stinking stuff. Maybe it was the smell that got rid of them. Whatever it was, the flies left or dropped dead on the floor.

Except for the cows, I was alone. The sound of Daddy's tractor was a long way away. I heard the gate to the lot swing open and shut.

Suddenly, two men stood in the doorway of the milk barn.

Chapter 2.

VISITORS

When I saw it was Stove Pipe and Nashville Ned, I wasn't too concerned. Mama wasn't with them, so I knew they had come straight to the barn. They knew when our chore time was.

Mama didn't like me being alone with the bo's. If she had known they were there, she would have come right out. Even though she preferred them to bums, she still said, "You never can tell about those guys."

Stove Pipe's real name was Arnold Slip. At least he said that's what it was. He was a strange looking man, unlike anybody I had ever seen, except maybe in a circus.

He was 6'4" tall and had a peg leg from the knee down. The peg was made out of catalpa wood. We never found out how he lost his leg.

He told us once, "I did something stupid and I don't want to talk about it."

Each time he came to us, he wore the same clean, though wrinkled, black suit, a white shirt, and a black bow tie--even on hot days. He wore a black top hat which made him look ten feet tall. His teeth were unusually white and straight. Between those white teeth he clenched a silver cigarette holder, but there was never a cigarette in it. He didn't smoke. His tanned, smallish square face, inset with tiny black eyes, sat firmly on his narrow shoulders under that hat. The reason we called him Stove Pipe was because he was built like one. The man was nineteen inches around the chest, nineteen inches around the waist, and nineteen inches around the hips. He was the skinniest person I had ever seen, and because of his build, he was quite frail. However, that didn't stop him from doing light jobs willingly.

Ever so neatly he had printed on a small piece of cardboard these words: "I clean and repair saddles and harnesses, empty mousetraps, sharpen saws, tell funny stories, teach any dog to do tricks, and I myself do magic tricks, can croak like a frog, clean eye glasses, polish shoes, wash dishes, cook Chinese food, pray over food, I make a good pot of coffee, and do many other chores." This card was always pulled from his pocket and handed to my mother. She knew it by heart.

As soon as the fall temperatures began to drop, Stove Pipe headed south. His body was too delicate to handle our severe Missouri winter.

Nashville Ned, from Tennessee of course, was rather plain next to Stove Pipe, but he, too, was built funny. The poor man's long legs did not match the rest of his body.

The first time I saw him I had to laugh. After a while I would catch myself staring at him, wondering how he got that way.

Ned had a ruddy complexion and a pot belly under his striped overalls. He had reddish-blonde hair. If the man had one endearing feature, it was his trusting blue eyes.

Since hobos were usually younger than they looked, we never tried to guess their age.

Neither of these two men ever stayed around more than a few days. Ned was a good farm hand. Daddy was glad to have him for a day or two.

He enjoyed playing ball with us kids and pitching horseshoes with my dad and his friends.

Once more, here they stood in my barn door. They'd be looking for work and some supper, no doubt. Both men had deep, raspy voices. Daddy said their vocal cords were probably lined with cinder dust from the railroad.

"Save some work for us, little gal," Ned said cheerfully, waiting politely to be invited in.

Stove Pipe looked at me and smiled. His teeth were still just as white as snow.

"Hello. I'm glad to see you." I said. I meant it. It was great to have some help.

Without having to ask, they told me they had just come from two week's work in Kansas City at the stockyards. Ned had worked there before. One of the regular workers had been hit by a cattle truck and was laid up. The bo's had taken his place, sharing the job.

Farmers having cattle, hogs, or sheep to sell shipped them by truck to Omaha or to the Kansas City stockyards. The stockyards were a large, sprawling place, with hundreds of holding pens ready for incoming livestock. Company buyers were on hand twenty-four hours a day to weigh the loads and make checks out to the owners.

Fortunately for the bo's, they had gotten to eat at the Golden Ox, located near the stockyards and famous for its Kansas City steak dinners. All you could eat for $1.25. My brothers had often told us about eating there when they trucked cattle to Kansas City. The dinner was served on a giant metal platter. It consisted of a generous dinner salad, a gigantic beef steak, a choice of potatoes and vegetables, all the coffee or pop you could drink, and pie and ice cream. Today the same dinner would cost at least $25.00.

The bo's lived a hard but interesting life.

A welcomed bit of breeze blew through the barn, cooling. I milked two cows while Ned milked one and Stove Pipe got started on Rosie. I gave him our gentle Jersey.

When we were down to the last two cows, I began carrying buckets of milk to the house. The cream separator was on the screened-in back porch. Mama was waiting for the milk.

Before it could be separated it had to be strained several times to remove any dust or dirt. Once strained, the separator did the job of taking the whole milk and separating the cream from it. We ended up with several buckets of milk containing almost no cream. That was the skimmed milk. The pure cream went into a five-gallon can to be sold.

We filled quart and pint bottles with whole milk, capped them with round cardboard caps, and put them into wire carriers to be delivered to the front porches of Watson. The price of the milk was ten cents a quart and five cents a pint. Daddy delivered the milk after he'd eaten supper. If he had to back to work in the field, my sisters did the delivery. Lucille would drive and Irene would set the milk on the front porches.

"There'll be two more for supper," I told Mom as I poured another bucket of fresh, warm milk into the large separator bowl. I didn't know any other girl my age that could even carry a three-and-a-half-gallon bucket of milk, let alone lift it over their head into a separator. I could carry two full buckets. I did it all the time. Sometimes I showed off and swung them over my head.

I hated the smell of warm milk. Yuck! How anybody could drink the stuff was beyond me. The barn cats got fat on it. Daddy and I figured that the cats deserved all the milk they could drink for keeping down the rodent population. We always had at least a dozen cats. There were three big pans in the milk barn, where the cats got all the milk they could drink. Sometimes, a cat would come and stand behind the cow I was milking and I would squirt milk right into its mouth. The cats loved it. If I wanted to get rid of one, I'd aim for its face.

"Who is here?" Mama asked, while capping the milk bottles.

"Two hobos," I answered. It frightened her. I shouldn't have said it so bluntly.

"It's O.K. Don't worry. It's only Ned and Stove Pipe," I answered. "They're finishing up the milking."

Mama looked toward the barn. I knew she felt uneasy. Hobos always made her uneasy.

"Well, I'm glad it's them. Take over for me here for a minute. I've got supper on the stove," she said. Mama still cooked on a wood cook stove. Whatever she had been cooking smelled good. As long as there were plenty of dill pickles, I'd be happy. I ate dill pickles with everything, even dessert. Mama said I made people sick, the way I ate. Ask me if I cared. They didn't have to watch!

Because of my love for pickles, I was always happy to see the cucumber vines in the garden producing in abundance. We made all kinds of pickles. Mama bought mixed pickling spices by the gallon. She made dills in ten gallon-crocks, all varieties. She canned some whole, some sliced, and some in chunks. She canned sweet pickles, small and medium-sized, and she made sweet pickle relish. When the wind was in the right direction, the neighbors knew Mama was making pickles. You could smell the pickling spices a long way off. Each batch had its own aroma. There was always the tangy scent of vinegar--add to that onions, garlic, and sugar, enough to set your teeth on edge. I remember cinnamon, cloves, allspice, bay leaf, ginger, and other spices. By the time the blend of all these reached your nose, something magical had taken place. It was the unforgettable bouquet of pickling season.

The meanest fit I ever saw my mother throw was when Buell Sharp's dog ran into our house and knocked her pickling spices into the slop (garbage) bucket. She whooped down on that mutt with her string mop. The poor thing was so scared it slid head first through the back screen door. That's the last we ever saw of him.

By the time I had carried the skimmed milk to the hogs and chickens, Daddy was coming in with Ned and Stove Pipe. That meant the milking was done and the cows had been turned out of the barn. Good! They'd saved me more work. I inwardly thanked them.

Irene had come home from her job and was setting the table. Lucille was frosting a cake. At our house everybody worked. Mom and Daddy started us out young. I heard Lucille say she was going to save a piece of the cake for her boyfriend.

She had been dating Irene's eighth grade teacher, Wayne Douglas. One of those days I planned to visit Irene's class to see if I could

discover what Lucille saw in him. Lucille
thought he was so smart. I didn't. How smart
could he be? He was from the city. Wait until he
came to see Lucille. I would give him a word he'd
never heard of. We would see how bright he was!

Daddy and the bo's washed up outside at the
water pump, our only water source. In those days
all our water had to be pumped up from out of
the well. Ours was a good one. The water was
clean and fresh. We would hang a bucket on the
spout and pump the handle up and down to
bring it up. We pumped all the water we used for
cooking, drinking, bathing, cleaning, washing and
rinsing the clothes, etc. The pump got a good
workout and so did we.

Mama had seen the men coming and hurried
out with soap and towels. Stove Pipe hung that
tall hat of his on a peg out on the porch when
they came in. His hair looked like it had been
dyed black. I wanted to ask him about it, but I
knew Mom would give me one of her "that-was-
a-dumb-thing-to-do" looks.

Supper was on the dining room table. Lots of
food on a lace table cloth with embroidered
napkins of muslin that Lucille had made. She had
a special talent for making beautiful things for
the table.

There was a big platter of chicken-fried beef steaks, American-fried potatoes, gravy, cooked cabbage, fruit salad, hot rolls, and two kinds of pickles. Lucille brought her cake in from the kitchen with one piece missing. The bo's were smiling.

Like I always had and without thinking, I left the table and went into the kitchen to pour myself a small bowl of light Karo syrup. I ate it with a spoon, with everything. This time I got that "that-was-a-dumb-thing-to-do" look from my mother. She said I'd make our guests sick with my strange eating habits. My family was used to me. I had a feeling that Ned and Stove Pipe had pretty strong stomachs after being on the road for so long. They both told Mama to let me enjoy my syrup.

Daddy asked the blessing on the food, to which Stove Pipe said "Amen" before digging in.

"Just a few more days of school," Irene announced.

"Then what?" Ned asked.

"Irene has plans," I teased.

"What plans?" Daddy asked, helping himself to a fistful of hot rolls.

The phone on the dining room wall rang, so Irene got out of explaining her secret.

Even though it wasn't our ring, we all listened

to see if our neighbor, Mrs. Harmon, was going to answer her phone.

Mama looked at the clock. "They aren't home. Emma said they were going to Tarkio to the show."

Watson's telephone company consisted of Mr. and Mrs. Bowers. Mrs. Bowers operated the switchboard in town and her husband did the installations and serviced all the lines.

You reached the operator by rotating the little crank on the side of the wooden wall phone. Mrs. Bowers answered, "Operator." You'd give her the name of the person with whom you wished to speak. She could connect your line with anyone else on her switchboard.

There were three families on our line. When one of us got a phone call, all three phones rang. We each had a different ring to know if it was our call or not. Two longs and a short ring was ours. Two longs and two shorts were for Harmons. Three shorts were for the third family. If we wanted to, we could listen in on each others' calls. If we wanted to make a call, we had to wait until no one was using the line.

The phone rang two more times for the Harmons. Lucille got up and took down the receiver.

"They've gone to the show," Lucille told the

caller. "Oh, hello Mrs. Hudson. Yes, this is Lucille. How are all those beautiful new puppies?" She talked for a few minutes before returning to the table.

"I'll bet they've gone to see *Gone with the Wind* again," Irene said. "That will make the third time."

"Well worth it," Ned replied.

"Where have you fellows been?" Daddy asked.

I already knew, so I didn't pay too much attention until they finished telling about their work at the stockyards. Then it began to get interesting.

"I wintered mostly at King's Ranch in Texas," Stove Pipe was saying. "Kicked around the South a bit. Repaired a ton of tack (leather harnesses) in Kentucky. Derby horses. Big place. One feller had enough horses to keep eight or ten trainers busy. Pay was good, too. Nice, comfortable bunk house and good grub. Offered me a full time job of keeping the saddles and harnesses in good shape. I was tempted--told him I'd study on it."

Ned winked at my dad. He had a question for his friend. "Does Elsie Norton still cook there?"

Stove Pipe grinned. "Yes she does, Ned. Hair's just as red, eyes just as green. But she's fat!"

"Shoot man, she's always been fat," Ned reminded him.

"I know that," Stove Pipe laughed, but that don't matter none. She's got that certain somethin' I tell ya. She knows the way to a man's heart."

"Yeah," Ned answered, "through his stomach!"

The bo's made us all laugh.

Ned had spent the winter in Florida orchards, trimming and raking, he said.

Neither one of them had a family of their own...so they said.

In those days I wondered whether Stove Pipe's children would be born with a wooden peg like his, if he ever had any.

Chapter 3.

BIRDS, MICE, AND BOYFRIENDS

Irene offered to fix Stove Pipe up with Miss Bently, the old maid school teacher who taught third grade. She was skinny, too, like the bo, but pretty--for a teacher.

I asked Miss Bently once if she would ever get married. Her reply was, "I've had one true love and that was enough for me."

Mama told me that Miss Bently had been engaged to Harold Bickel. They got into a week-long fight. He wanted to marry her and move in with his parents. She wouldn't do it. Bickels were not very clean. Mama said the Bickels' house was always dirty. She said it was the kind that made you have to clean your feet when you came out instead of when you went in. My mother didn't usually say bad things about people, so I thought that was pretty funny.

30

Lucille and Irene had to wash the supper dishes. Mom always did the breakfast and dinner (noon) dishes. Because I worked so hard outside, I seldom had to work in the house, although I did every now and then to help Mama.

My sisters always argued when they were in the kitchen together. They argued about everything. They argued about who would wash and who would dry. Lucille would be mad because Irene had worn her sweater or blouse again, without asking. They argued about who the best-looking boys in school were. Lucille would tell Irene that her boyfriend looked like a sick groundhog. Irene would tell Lucille that her boyfriend was a big sissy, etc. I agreed with that.

Finally, Mom or Daddy would have enough. One of them would say, "Stop the arguing and get your work done."

One night, my sisters were going to make me wash the dishes after Daddy and I had been in the hay field all day. Both of them pushed and shoved but they couldn't get me into the kitchen. Finally, I sat down on the floor and started laughing so hard that they left me alone. Then, just for the fun of it, I went into our bedroom and sewed the sleeves of their nightgowns shut. When they found out, they both came after me with pillows. It was all in fun.

We had no indoor plumbing. There was neither indoor bathroom nor running water in the house. For us, everything took a bit longer. Water had to be carried in by the bucket-full from the well. If you wanted hot water, it had to be heated on Mama's wood cook stove in the kitchen. Before that, there had to be fuel carried in to heat it. We used dried corn cobs and thin sticks of wood for kindling and bigger sticks to keep the fire going. Another of my daily chores was to carry in a basket of cobs and several arm-loads of wood for the kitchen stove.

While my sisters did the dishes and there was still daylight, I had birds to kill. Literally. Daddy paid me a penny a piece for every sparrow I shot. It was a bumper year for sparrows. Hundreds of the nasty buggers flew around the barn. Daddy said their droppings on the hay and grain could not be tolerated. So, I went hunting with my trusty Daisy B-B gun.

I had several tried and true spots from which to do my shooting. But from wherever I stood, the cats stole from me. As soon as a bird hit the ground, one of the cats would snatch it in its teeth and run. It was not unusual for two or three cats to fight over the same bird. When that happened, I'd throw them each a bird from my bucket just to get rid of them. I had to keep a close eye on my catch.

Twenty-seven dead birds later, I decided to shoot three more for an even thirty. Every penny counted. Maybe someday, if Daddy would let me, I would buy a dog. Not just any dog, either. A fine stock dog that would save me time and lots of steps. There was nothing I wanted more than a dog. I begged, but no one listened.

Before I went back to the house, I filled the mangers with more ground hay and put corn into the feed boxes for the next day. The ground hay was nearly weightless. By putting one basket on top of the other, I could carry two at a time.

The hay smelled sweet. It took about fifteen trips from the metal bins to fill the mangers. Nothing had a finer aroma than freshly cut alfalfa hay. Farmers mowed their hay and let it dry a day or two before putting it into a barn loft or on a stack. That wonderful scent permeated the air for miles around. City folks took drives in the country in the evening with their windows rolled down, just to get a whiff of the new mown hay. We should have charged them for the privilege.

Filling the feed boxes with corn was heavier work. For that reason, the storage building had been built next to the milk barn.

When I opened the door, there was a mouse

running around on top of the corn. Nasty thing! I closed the door and called, "Here kitty kitty!" A willing, yellow barn cat came running. I reached down, picked him up, opened the door, and tossed him inside. I leaned my back up against the door and folded my arms. The wait was short. The cat snarled on the other side. Then I thought it was over. I opened the door and out he jumped, with a dead mouse dangling from his jaws. The proud feline strolled by several onlooking cats, growling a warning.

I had been wrong. The job was not over. The next time I opened the door, there were three or four more mice running close to the walls. I opened the door wide and called for cats. Immediately they understood their responsibility. The poor mice didn't have a chance.

By the time the bird-hunting and the cat and mouse game was over, I had tired of the idea of filling the corn boxes. However, I was committed, so I completed the job quickly. I didn't want to miss Lucille's boyfriend. Like Irene, I thought he was a real sissy. But, because he was Irene's teacher, she said I had to call him "Mr. Douglas." Lucille loved him. She made me sick, the way she moon-eyed him.

They were sitting close together on the front porch swing. So, naturally, I headed for the front porch.

Mr. Douglas smiled at me. "Hi Colene! How's my favorite girl?" Yuck! I didn't answer.

"What ya been doin', Tootie?" Lucille asked. She never called me by my real name; she and Daddy always called me "Tootie."

"Been killing birds. Got a full bucket of barn sparrows and four dead mice for Mama to cook up for breakfast in the morning," I said seriously, hoping to shake up the city boy.

I did. Mr. Lover Boy held his stomach and turned pale.

Lucille was used to me. She didn't notice her boyfriend was about ready to throw up.

"Look what Wayne brought me, Tootie," she smiled, holding up an eight by ten glossy photo of Clark Gable. *Not only* did she love Mr. Douglas, she loved Mr. Gable as well, a hand- some movie star who had starred in the movie *Gone With the Wind.*

"Oh, how conthreating!" I replied, using one of my "just-made-it-up-for-the-fun-of-it" words.

Mr. Douglas, still pale from my remark about the birds and mice, repeated my "word" with a strange look on his face. He was still holding his stomach and had stopped the swing.

Having done all the damage I could do, I left them alone.

Mr. Douglas was no Clark Gable, I could tell you that.

Lucille told me several days later that Mr. Douglas had looked in his big Webster's Dictionary to find "conthreating." Naturally, it hadn't been there. I had to laugh. When I became a professional writer someday, I'd have to remember not to use that word.

The bo's had decided to sleep in the barn and do the milking for me the next morning. I got to sleep until 7:30. Just because I missed two hours of milking cows didn't mean I got out of work, though. Mama made me rake up the chicken droppings under the roost in the hen house before I left for school. I wasn't too happy about starting my day off by raking up manure.

I probably went to school smelling like chicken poop!

Chapter 4.

GETTING EVEN

I couldn't believe what happened to me at school. By the time I got home, my head hurt so bad, I was sick.

Thomas, a boy in my class--the one who went around telling everybody he loved me, (Yuck!), hit me over the head as hard as he could with three heavy books. He took me by surprise! I just stood there. My legs felt like rubber. Everything went black. For a moment I couldn't see. I grabbed hold of the stairway banister to stay on my feet. Why had he done this to me?

I heard one of the girls say, "Thomas, when Mrs. Landon hears about this, she'll whip you for sure."

Thomas turned pale. "I didn't mean to hit her so hard."

Without a word, I staggered out the front door

of the school house. I was embarrassed and afraid I'd cry. But I didn't.

I was half way home before my vision cleared. I felt like I'd been kicked by a mule. Every step jarred my head.

Mom was not in the house. I changed my clothes to go to the barn. It didn't matter if I was healthy or gut-puke sick, I had chores to do. The milk buckets were missing from the porch. That meant the bo's were still around and helping out. There must have been a God after all.

I headed for the barn to help. Ned told me that Daddy was reseeding one of the hay fields. Mama had gone down to take him a drink of water.

Ned and Stove Pipe had the cows in the barn and were just getting started with the milking. I suffered through it. I didn't tell anybody about my aching head until we sat down at the supper table. As soon as Mama took a look at me, she knew something was wrong.

I told them how it happened and added, "I didn't cry, Daddy." My family considered it sissified to cry.

"Well, I'll take care of that young pup as soon as I finish eating my supper," Daddy said angrily--just like I knew he would.

Ned looked first at Daddy and then at me. "How big is this kid, Colene?"

"About the same size as me--maybe a little taller," I answered.

"Could you handle him?" Stove Pipe asked.

Mama didn't like that. "Now, I don't want my daughter to start a fight."

"Too late, Mom. He started it, not me. Stove Pipe is right. I could handle that kid any day of the week. Please, don't do anything, Daddy. Let me." I took two Bayer aspirin tablets and headed for the canvas hammock under the walnut tree. I hoped my head would soon stop throbbing! After a while I felt better and slept for about an hour. By the time I woke up, some of the pain had gone away. Daddy and the bo's were sitting on the porch, visiting.

Daddy got called to the phone.

Stove Pipe came over to the hammock. "Little gal, maybe I was wrong in figuring you to get back at that kid," he said earnestly. "How ya feeling?"

"Better. It wouldn't have mattered to me who told me to get him or not to get him--I'm gonna make Thomas wish he had never been born." I laughed and when I did, I felt a goose egg had swollen up on my sore head. I couldn't let Mama find out. She would keep me home from school.

Ned told me that he and Stove Pipe had planned to catch the early 5:27 freight in the morning. They wanted to do my chores for me, though, so they'd catch the 10:30 instead. Daddy told me later that they were heading for Iowa to put flowers on an old friend's grave.

Stove Pipe gave me a piece of advice. "Arm yourself with one big book. Didn't he hit you with books? Then catch him by surprise. Didn't he catch *you* by surprise? Then, if I was you, I'd scat." The bo laughed. "And, watch your back, little gal."

The bo worried about me. I liked that.

Armed with our 12" x 15", hardbound atlas, I headed to school with a confident grin on my face. I caught up with Iva and Laura at the railroad tracks.

"Whatcha doin' with that big book, Colene?" Iva grinned.

Laura looked at me and laughed. "You're gonna hit him, aren't you?"

"Don't say anything to anybody. O.K.?" I asked.

Thomas always beat me to school, but this morning he was nowhere to be seen. Darn! Now what? I intended to get him before school, first thing.

We had to go past the band room before we

got to our classroom. The band room was empty. I slipped in there to wait. A couple of minutes later, I saw Thomas pass by the window. His hands were rammed deep in his pants pockets. I heard him say confidently to Gerald, "I ain't afraid of no girl."

I waited until he came into view. Quickly, I jumped out in front of him as he had done to me. With both hands gripping my heavy book, I slammed it down hard on his head. Since his hands were still in his pockets, he fell flat on his face. He raised his head and looked dazed. I knew the feeling and it wasn't a good one.

"Well, you'd better be afraid of this girl, Thomas. Now we're even and if you ever lay a hand on me again, I'll sick my hobo friends on you."

Thomas had blood flowing from his nose and a bruised cheek where he had hit the floor. Not used to being cruel to anyone, I felt sorry for him. I offered my hand to help him up. He surprised all the kids watching by accepting it.

"I don't know why I hit you yesterday. It was a dumb thing to do," he said sheepishly. "I'm sorry. When Mrs. Landon sees this bloody shirt, I'll be in trouble for sure. I don't hate you or anything like that."

"No, Thomas loves you, Colene," one of the

boys teased. Thomas gave him a shove.

The five-minute bell sounded. It was over. I'd gotten even. Maybe it was wrong to feel as good about it as I did.

Mrs. Landon *did* ask Thomas about the blood on his shirt. He lied and told her that he had buried a dead cat that had been run over in front of his house and hadn't had time to go back and change his shirt. Everybody laughed, even the kids who knew he was lying.

Later, at home, I thought I'd better tell my folks.

"The bo's will be back in a couple of weeks," Daddy said. "They'll want to hear how you handled Thomas."

"I cleaned his clock and gave him a headache like he gave me!" I said, before filling them in on all the details of the incident.

Mama threw a fit just like I knew she would. "Why can't you act like a young lady? Mrs. Landon would have handled it."

"But, just look at all the fun I'd have missed out on," I laughed.

"Come on, Mom. You know you like getting even. Remember what River Johnny says: `Don't get mad, get even.'"

Mama just shook her head. "I swear, you remember everything those hobos say."

She was right. I had learned a lot from the bo's. They knew how to survive. Much of what I'd heard them say, I had tucked away in my head for future use.

Chapter 5.

CHICKENS, CUTS, AND CYCLONES

Lucille graduated from high school. Mr. Douglas moved back to Iowa for the summer. So, right away my sister got herself some new boyfriends--thank goodness!

Unfortunately, one of them drove too fast. This one was from Fairfax. He and Lucille, along with another couple, were on their way to see a first-run movie called *The Wizard of Oz*. Lucille's new boyfriend was driving. He took the infamous Herron Curve at about seventy miles an hour. His already dented 1935 Ford rolled over and over into a ditch. While the car was rolling over, Lucille's door flew open and she was thrown out. The car passed over her before it came to a stop.

Mrs. Bowers heard Mr. Herron's call to

Doctor Gray. Knowing that Mama and Daddy would want to know, she rang our number. Mama was scared to death. She told Daddy, "If a car rolls over you, you're dead." Mama was wrong.

My sister was lucky. She was not killed. In fact, she didn't even get a single broken bone. What she did get were two black eyes and lots of cuts and bruises. She couldn't walk for two weeks. Nobody else in the car had even gotten a scratch.

Lucille's lousy new boyfriend didn't come to see her or call to see how she was doing. Not once! Maybe he was afraid of Daddy. Another guy came instead. He hung around all the time until Daddy ran him off.

When Lucille graduated from high school, Irene graduated from the eighth grade. Irene had long red hair and blue eyes. She was really pretty. Guys looked at her a lot. Mama didn't like it.

Irene helped Daddy, too, when she wasn't working at the store. I couldn't help feeling sorry for her. She wasn't used to the work. She seldom had to milk cows, but she helped pull hay off the tall stacks for the grinding. There was plenty of work to go around. Daddy and Mom should have had more boys, or got into a business that required girls. But, alas, my dad was a farmer.

It was Mama who managed the chickens. She took pride in her responsibility. This year was no different than any other. Mama bought five-hundred day-old chicks.

The brooder house was cleaned and disinfected for their arrival. The building was small, yet adequate. In the center, there was an oil heater and a metal umbrella that hovered over the chicks to keep them warm.

These soft, yellow babies came by train from Earl May's Seed Company in Shenandoah, Iowa. There were one-hundred chicks to a box. All made happy "cheeping" sounds. The boxes had many holes in them, about the size of a penny, so the chicks could breathe.

Mama practically lived with them at first. If they bunched up, they'd smother and die. So, we took turns going out to the brooder house to "stir the chicks." In other words, we had to keep them separated. The chicks had a habit of crowding together. If they were to be saved, they had to be pushed apart. Mama invented the phrase, "stirring the chicks."

It was May and time to plant another big garden. Mama fed half of Watson. She gave food to everybody who visited us.

There was a sign by our front gate that read,

"Cold milk for sale." People stopped to buy milk. When they did, Mama would give them some of whatever was available from the garden. There was so much food, we never missed it.

In those days, we had an ice box to keep our food and milk cold. The ice man came a couple of times a week. We bought fifty-pound chunks of ice to refrigerate the box. If we wanted ice for drinks, it had to be chipped off with an ice pick.

Besides the garden, there had been a half-acre of potatoes planted on March 17th. Daddy always planted potatoes on St. Patrick's day, unless it was too wet to plow the ground.

Something really funny had happened in Watson on St. Patrick's Day.

There was a Bemberger family who lived just outside of Watson. Mr. Bemberger drove a truck that had his first initials, "C.H.," on the door. Because he always hauled corn in that truck, we always called him "Corn Hauling" Bemberger.

The Bembergers, at that time, had six-year-old twin boys. On St. Patrick's Day, the twins drove their dad's corn-hauling truck to town and slammed it right into the post office building on Main Street.

Trudie, the Postmistress, telephoned their mother. Trudie told her that she could only see one head. One of them was steering and the other was on the floor pushing on the gas and the brake.

The twins were always in trouble. Not long before that, one of them had gotten up on the clothesline post, fallen off, and broken his arm. The other twin climbed up to the same place, hoping to fall and break his arm, too. Luckily, he didn't.

Daddy saw the Bemberger family in Dr. Gray's office when the boy's broken arm was in a plaster cast. These six-year-old boys had gotten into a fist fight and started cussing each other. Their dad just laughed and let them fight it out. He said he knew they'd quit when they got tired.

The Bembergers were sure different than my mom and dad. They did not allow cussing and arguing, unless they were doing the arguing.

Daddy was a Democrat. It was always President Roosevelt this and President Roosevelt that. Mama was a Republican. She hated Roosevelt. Mama said he would get us into war with Hitler. My parents fought day and night about politics.

Politics weren't the only thing they disagreed about. Mama didn't like it when Daddy gave our town enough land to build a baseball diamond back behind our alfalfa field. He loved baseball. Watson had a good town team, but no proper place to play. Daddy cut all the weeds and grass and scraped the area to get it into shape. He even fenced it with new fencing. The town raised enough money to put up lights and a snack shack. Mama said all those cars coming into our driveway would throw more dirt in the house and scare our cows.

Long about that time I started working in the fields for Daddy. Mama wasn't too keen on that, either. But, Irene and I were the only help he had, and she also had her work at the store.

We had a tractor, two teams of horses, and one team of mules. I knew how to harness the teams, but I had to stand on a box to throw the heavy leather harnesses over their backs. Hitching them up to the wagons and machinery was easy for me.

One job I got tired of was grinding corn for the milk cows. First, I had to hitch up the tractor to a wood wagon. Then, I had to drive to the corn crib and fill the wagon with ear corn. It was heavy work. Next, I'd haul the load of corn over to the crib where we kept the ground corn. There was a grinder there, just outside the barn lot. A wide belt hitched up to the fly wheel on the tractor made the grinder work. I shovelled the corn into the grinder hopper, one heavy scoop-full at a time, until it was all ground. I was thankful for the blower that blew the ground corn, cobs and all, into the crib. When the crib began to look empty, the job of grinding had to be done all over again. When Daddy was not working in the fields, he did the grinding. Sometimes I helped and sometimes Irene did, too. Three was better than two.

After the grinding was done, I had about twenty minutes for reading.

There was a new book out called *The Yearling,* by Marjorie Rawlings. I loved it. It was about a boy who had a deer for a pet. I hoped the story wasn't true because it was so sad and made me cry. Mrs. Rawlings got the Pulitzer Prize for fiction that year.

Next to writing, I liked to read best. However, both activities were always interrupted by my mother's complaining.

Mama sympathized with the poor people who had to look to the government kitchens for a meal. These were public soup kitchens. Times were hard since the Depression. Mama blamed Roosevelt for that, too. I thought Mama was wrong. At least the hungry were getting fed. I had heard the bo's talk about soup kitchens and I never heard them complain. Some days that was all they had.

I *did* hear several bo's tell Mama that her food was a lot better than what they'd had in the soup kitchens, though.

Over a month had passed and Ned and Stove Pipe had not been back. That meant they'd found work.

There were very few women hobos. Mama liked it when Missouri Minnie came. She washed windows. Minnie wore white coveralls. Her pockets were filled with clean rags and a cake of Bonami to clean with.

Bonami was a hard, white bar of window soap. You rubbed the bar with a wet cloth, then spread it on the window to let it dry. It dried to a powder in about a minute. Once it was wiped off, the glass was sparkling clean.

Minnie had coal black hair and a crooked nose. Some crazy drunk woman had pushed her out of a box car. Hitting the ground, she'd broken her nose and bruised her face. She told us if she ever ran in to that old heifer on a freight again, she would slam a box car door on her-- right between her shoulders and her ears.

Mama was fond of Minnie. She told her she hoped she'd find that "old heifer" one day. Mama always gave her money and food and sometimes clothes if she needed them. The bo's who knew Minnie said she was a real lady. Minnie said the other hobos were generally kind to her.

California Carl and River Johnny were with us for several days, this time, helping Daddy with some fencing and repair work on the milk barn. River Johnny was a good carpenter. These two bo's were more educated. Carl reminded me of a banker.

One day while they were with us, they saw me working on Daddy's disc. A disc is a long piece of machinery with lots of round blades. We used it on plowed ground to cut up the clods and smooth out the soil.

We called our Missouri soil "gumbo." Actually, it was sandy loam. The best in the midwest. When our gumbo soil got wet, it was almost like gum and it stuck to everything, including this disc.

Anyway, Daddy said he was through with the disc for a while. My job was to get all the dirt off of it and put it away. I hated cleaning the disc. There were about thirty of those 18" round blades. They were sharp and close together. I had to clean each blade off with a wooden paddle, then rub each one with sandpaper. After that, a coat of axle grease was smeared on with a brush to keep it from rusting. I would cut my hands in several places every time on those sharp blades.

"Why are you doing that?" California Carl

asked when he saw me there.

"Because my dad told me to," I answered.

"Your Daddy needs to get himself some more help, I'm thinking," River Johnny said, looking at his partner.

"Well, I'm it," I said.

I was about half finished with the disc. My hands were bleeding from cuts and scrapes and were getting sore as the dickens.

The bo's picked up my sandpaper and the paint brush and told me to go play with my friends.

It didn't take me long to say thanks and get away fast.

I headed to the house to wash up and put Cloverine salve on my cuts. I was heading out the door when Mama caught me.

"Colene, is that you? Did you get the disc put away? I need you to pick some peas from the garden. We'll have new potatoes and peas with supper, O.K.?"

Even though I wanted to tell her no, "no" wasn't a word I ever said to my parents. It was not allowed.

My hands were so sore, it took a while to pick enough peas for our supper. Mama hollered at me a couple of times to hurry, but I didn't care. I just let her yell. I was tired and there was still milking to do. While I was in the garden, the wind came up and began to whip things around. Dark clouds were gathering. It looked and smelled like a cyclone was coming.

After the pea-picking, Mama sent me to the machine shop to get her a hammer. The bo's had just finished up the disc.

"Didn't you get to play, honey?" Carl asked.

"No sir, I picked peas for Mama for supper," I answered.

"Didn't you tell her about your sore hands?" he asked.

"What difference would that make? I'd have to do it anyhow." I told them. "Have you seen my dad?"

Johnny pointed toward the implement shed. "He said something about grinding hay. I think he went to pull hay from the big stack."

I returned to my mother with the hammer. I figured the bo's would go help my dad take hay from the stack. If they did, he'd have help with the grinding. I knew I'd be doing all the milking. Thanks to the bo's, at least the hay-grinding would get done while I milked the cows.

I gathered the milk buckets and headed to the barn. I took a minute to stop by the machine shed and check out three new baby kittens.

The cows were more than a half-mile away and

with the wind howling, they would never hear my voice. Our farm was four-hundred acres. It was nearly three-and-half miles around the perimeter.

I supposed I'd be dead and gone and never know what it was like to have had the help of a good stock dog to help me with my chores.

By the time I finished milking and was carrying two heavy buckets of milk to the house, the wind was so strong it was pushing me. A cardboard box went flying across to the chickenyard fence. It scared the hens so much that they were squawking and jumping around. I hoped they'd have sense enough to get in the chicken house. Our chickens were so stupid.

Daddy and the bo's had to stop working with the hay. The wind blew it off the wagon as fast as they put it on.

Before a cyclone, the sky turned yellow for a few minutes, and that's what it was doing now.

Mom was herding everybody to the underground cellar. When the cyclones came, the only safe place was the cellar, because the wind could blow the roof off the house, or worse.

The storm was loud. For about twenty minutes, great gusts of wind slammed against the cellar door. We covered our ears against the great claps of thunder coming from the clouds that had turned black right above our house. Lightning ripped across the sky. This time, the rain passed us by. Mama was frightened. She leaned against the potato bins there in the cellar and wrapped her arms in her long apron.

As the cyclone moved on, one by one we left the cellar, surveying our home for signs of destruction. This time we were fortunate. Our place had suffered minimal damage. The back screen door had blown open and hung on one hinge. But that was it.

Later that evening, our neighbor stopped by to tell us that he had lost a productive milk cow to the storm. Lightning had killed her when she took shelter under a maple tree. We were all sorry for his loss.

After supper, Iva and Laura came over to play cards with me and my family. I fell asleep in Daddy's red leather chair. Suddenly, I heard two longs, a short, and another long toot from a freight train whistle. I knew the signals. The train would be stopping in Watson. Then I heard one short toot for brakes. Unusual for a freight to be stopping in Watson so late.

Ten minutes passed and another hobo stood at our kitchen door. It was Walkabout Tommy, a man who claimed to be from Texas. He said hello to everyone and slapped Carl and Johnny on the back. Daddy went to his desk drawer, pulled out an envelope and handed it to him. Tommy did not ask for food, but said goodbye to us and left.

I dared not ask my father. But I sure would've liked to know what was in that envelope.

Chapter 6.

A CHRISTMAS TO FORGET

As long as I live, I will never forget my Christmas of 1939. I was ten years old and looking forward to the holidays and Christmas presents just like any other ten-year-old kid. Unlike Watson's, Rock Port's streets and stores were decorated with Christmas lights.

I never had very much money, but I always bought a small gift for everyone in my family. All through the year, when we shopped in Rock Port on Saturday night, I'd spend time at the dime store. In those days, twenty-five cents would buy ten times as much as it does now.

Every Saturday night we went to Rock Port to do our trading. Everybody did. We bought and sold. Mama sold eggs. She took from thirty to sixty dozen eggs in wooden crates. She bought chicken feed in cloth sacks and used the material to make clothes and aprons. The produce companies who prepared the chicken feed were smart enough to use attractive material for their sacks. When Mama picked out her chicken feed, it was the material she was interested in as much as the feed. She might ask for two bags in the green and yellow daisy material and two more in the pink and white striped bags. Mama was a good customer, not to mention one of the prettiest. The store owners appreciated her business.

Later, she shopped for groceries while Daddy visited with other farmers and shopped at the hardware store. He always bought a bag of candy and a newspaper. A couple of times I saw Mama in the dime store, but I always stayed away from her, thinking she might be buying Christmas presents for me.

I loved the Christmas carols on the radio and at church. The week before Christmas, my friends and I would go from door to door in the evening, singing Christmas carols. I knew all the verses of every carol. We never passed up families who gave us fudge and donuts. We knew who lived in every house in Watson.

When the moon was shining bright and there was snow crunching underneath our feet, we didn't mind the cold at all. It was like a winter wonderland.

I was ten years old, but I knew about Santa Claus already. Nobody told me. I figured it out one night at our local grocery store when Santa paid a visit there. Through the cheap mask, I saw Glenn Ellison's eyes. I remember being very disappointed.

At last, Christmas morning arrived. Daddy didn't wake me up to go to the milk barn. That part was O.K.. When I got up, it was late-- probably about 7:30. My mom and dad, my brother Charley, and my sisters were still at the dining room table, finishing up breakfast.

When I went into the room, no one spoke to me. I thought they were going to surprise me or something. I was the youngest. No one said "good morning," "Merry Christmas," or anything. My plate was there and food was still on the table. There was sausage, scrambled eggs, fried potatoes, gravy, and biscuits.

It was not unusual for my family not to talk to me, or even listen to me, for that matter. When I said anything, it was like they all turned deaf.

While I ate, I listened to Charley and Lucille talk about a Christmas Eve party they had attended the night before. Everybody seemed to be having a good time at the table. Gifts, empty boxes and wrapping paper were piled here and there on the table and the sideboard. Irene showed me her new blouse and manicure set from the folks. Lucille had been given the same. I also saw a new sweater, some jewelry, a scarf, a book and several other things, but I didn't know whose they were. There were other gifts from them to each other, beautifully wrapped in colorful paper and ribbon.

Charley had a new shirt and tie in a box and a set of playing cards with pretty girls on them. Some unopened packages were leaning against his chair.

I saw that the new pipe I had wrapped for my dad was lying by his plate. Seeing the pipe, I was sure their presents from me had been opened.

Finally, I asked. "Do I have any presents?"

Mom said, "In the front room on the chair."

When I looked where she pointed, I saw a small coloring book, meant for a four- or five-year-old child, and a small box of crayons.

She surely didn't mean these things, I thought.

"Where did you say my presents were, Mom?" I asked again.

"I told you, right there on the chair." She pointed to the coloring book and crayons.

Why was she being so cranky with me?

"Thank you," I said. I looked more closely at the coloring book to see if there was something inside it, but there wasn't. I felt empty and hurt, but I didn't say anything. Even though I was used to being left out, this was wrong.

I put on my coat, went outside, and sat in Charley's truck, trying not to cry. I tried to understand. I guess I thought parents treated their children equally, especially at Christmas. I really didn't need anything. But it *was* Christmas. I had been swept under the rug and forgotten about? Why?

I felt lost not having to do the milking. But I wasn't too thrilled about sitting there in the truck. It was cold, not more than 10 or 15 degrees, and there was snow on the ground. I wanted something to keep me busy for a while. There was always wood to be carried in for the heating stoves. I got out the sled and went to work. I piled the porch with as much wood as would fit. I was wondering what I could do next, but I was getting cold.

Charley came out, all dressed up to go someplace. He was twenty-four--fourteen years older than me. Sometimes he seemed more like an uncle than a brother.

"Don't you know it's Christmas?" he asked. "You shouldn't be working so hard."

I had never seen him carry in a stick of wood in my life.

"Really?" I asked. "Then why don't you carry in the wood?" He didn't answer. "What did you get for Christmas? And did you like what I gave you?" I asked.

"Let's see, you gave me the box of handkerchiefs with my initials in the corner, right?" he asked.

"What else did you get?" I asked.

He named off a lot of presents, from the family and friends.

"Well, I guess you guys all care for each other a lot. I don't know what else to do to make you like me. I work as hard as I know how to help out. I never cause trouble. Mom and Daddy gave me a coloring book meant for a little kid and a small box of crayons. I guess I'm just feeling sorry for myself because rest of you got so many nice gifts, and I didn't." I told him.

My brother got a real strange look on his face. He reached down and gave me a hug and went flying into the house. Almost immediately, I could hear my family shouting at each other. Daddy was yelling the loudest. Something about Mama always buying the presents, so it was her fault I was overlooked.

I went in, wanting to hear what they were saying, but they all shut up.

"See Charley, nobody even wants to talk to

me. It's O.K., you guys. I don't need presents. All I ever asked for was a puppy to train as a stock dog to make my work a little easier. But I know I'll never get one," I told them.

For some reason, my sisters left the room crying. Maybe I had touched a nerve. Mom and Daddy just glared at each other.

"I'm sorry we've ruined your Christmas, Sis," Charley said. "If Mom and Daddy won't get you that puppy, I will. I know how much work you do." He looked at his watch and left.

As it turned out, my family all tried to be nice to me for the next few days. Daddy took me to the store the day after Christmas and bought me a toy typewriter. But it wasn't the same as getting it on Christmas morning. Charley never again mentioned a puppy.

Every night I dreamed about dogs, all kinds. I dreamed about beautiful, well-trained stock dogs and I dreamed about wild, ugly dogs, who ran the cattle through the fence, ripping their flesh. I saw blood spurting out where milk should be. To make myself quit dreaming, I'd get out of bed and stand up to stay awake, until I got so cold that I had to get back under the covers.

The week after Christmas, Daddy and a couple of our neighbor men butchered several hogs. Three were ours. It was a bloody job. First they had to kill the hogs, then scald them in a long tub of hot water. Next, all the hair had to be scraped off. The hogs were hung up by their two hind legs, cut open from their neck to their tail on the underside and everything was removed that was not fit to eat.

We sugar-cured the hams and wrapped them to hang in the smoke house. Most of the meat had to be cut into roasts, chops, ribs, etc., and wrapped before it was taken to a rented frozen food locker in town. All the small meat was ground into sausage. The worst job was cleaning up the mess, both indoors and out.

On butchering day, Mama always cooked up some of the fresh tenderloin for supper. It was the best cutting of meat. Tenderloin is the pork loin chop, minus the bone. It was fried in lard, and it was wonderful. With it, we had mashed potatoes, gravy, hot biscuits, vegetables from the cellar, hot apple pie, and store-bought ice cream. It was the kind of meal that city folks dream about.

The next day, after all the fat had been cut into pieces, we dumped it into a big black pot and built a fire under it out in the yard. When it liquified, it separated into a mixture of lard and pork rinds, with the rinds floating on top. The rinds are the hide of the hog. When cooked up with lard, they become crunchy and irresistibly delicious. Today you can buy them in the supermarket, but they are not as good.

The lard was ladled into syrup buckets for Mama's kitchen and stored in the cellar. In those days, everybody cooked with lard. We ate a lot of fried food. Mama used it for baking and for anything that called for shortening. Popcorn tastes better cooked in lard than anything else.

No matter how busy we were, the war in Europe was always on our minds. Mama brought us up to date by saying that the war news from Europe was not good. She said somebody ought to kill that "paper-hanging" Hitler. Before Hitler had become a dictator, he'd hung wallpaper. I found that pretty funny.

Mama was mad at Roosevelt again, too. She said he had the Japanese mad at us. Daddy told her not to worry, we were too powerful a country to be afraid of Japan. He said they would never cause us trouble. Time would tell.

Work on the farm in the winter was sometimes torturous. The cows still had to be milked twice a day. With no work in the fields, Daddy did a lot of the milking. I still got the job of going after the cows, even in the snow. The winter weather made all the work more unpleasant. There was still corn and hay to prepare, hogs to feed and water, and firewood, water, and cobs to be carried into the house. Days were shorter. Most of the choring was done in the dark.

A kerosine tank heater kept the stock tank from freezing, so the cows and horses had water. Before we got the tank heater, Irene and I had to go out and break ice so the animals could drink. Sometimes, when the tank froze solid, we had to carry buckets of water from the well to the livestock. It was a cold job.

Looking toward spring, Daddy bought another tractor. This one was bigger and more powerful. It was an "M" Farmal. Having two meant we'd have one a piece.

More time on the tractor for me meant more worry for Mama.

Chapter 7.

1940 - SPRING AND SUMMER

Spring came suddenly. One day the snow melted and the Missouri River flooded out of its banks. The Army came to fill sand bags and help keep the river from flooding Watson. The river bottom farmers always got flooded. We never did.

In spite of all the trouble, my family took time out for some rest and relaxation.

There was a new Disney movie out called *Fantasia*. On Sunday afternoons we made a habit of going to Rock Port to the matinee. We were Baptist and weren't supposed to do that on Sundays, so our preacher didn't like it. But, we went anyway.

Warmer weather brought more hobos up from the south. Mickey Munduco and Appalachia Man came in April. Others came before them, but I don't remember their names.

Mickey Munduco was handsome, for a hobo. Daddy said he looked like a gypsy and dressed like one. He wasn't a gypsy, though. He was Cajun. I loved to hear him sing French-Cajun songs. He wore a small, round accordion, suspended from his shoulder by a wide yellow strap. He played it to accompany his singing. Any time he felt like it, he'd sing. He loved to entertain. To make money, he stopped on the street, put his hat upside down on the sidewalk, and began entertaining. People stood and listened and put money in his hat. I thought that was a strange way of making money. Once, I told him so. He just laughed and said, "It may seem strange to you, but it is quite natural for me and it is so easy."

Appalachia Man said he was from Louisiana. He was tall and skinny, used glasses, and wore boots made out of alligator skin.

He said at that time America had two million freight cars in use. He told us a true story about how the railroad companies kept track of them:

One Sunday evening in California, a steel drum filled with chemicals blew sky high. Something had gone wrong in the mixing. Soon after they were put into drums, the chemicals expanded. Somewhere in the U.S. there were five separate car loads of drums on trains. They had to be located fast before they, too, exploded. By use of punched cards, sorting and tabulating machines, Teletypes, and mail reports from other railroads, the cars were located in ninety minutes. Each car was numbered. The five box cars were in five states: New Jersey, California, Iowa, Nevada and Illinois. Luckily, they were found in time so the drums could be depressurized to avoid more explosions.

Quite a story.

By July 1st, our green beans were ready for canning. Stove Pipe showed up to help with the breaking and bottling. It was a job he loved. Every year, Mama put up four or five-hundred quarts. She packed that cellar so full, there was hardly room left to walk. What we didn't grow in the garden to bottle, she traded for. If our tomato plants didn't produce enough for our table and the canning, she traded strawberries for more tomatoes from Mr. Beauty. She traded our surplus of blue concord grapes for apples. In the summer and fall, we ate from the garden. In the winter and spring, we ate from the cellar. There was plenty of food.

The day when Mom, Iva, Laura, and I were in the garden picking peas, Mr. Hudson came by on his bicycle. He was all excited about television.

He seemed to know a lot more about it than we did. I think his wants were premature, since it was another five or ten years before any of us ever saw a television.

One day in August, my family got up early and drove to the rodeo in Sidney, Iowa. I always felt sorry for the poor cowboys when they got bucked off the wild, longhorned bulls. At least one of the them always got hurt. Our day at the rodeo was the one day of the year that Daddy hired the milking done.

On the way to the rodeo, Mama did not speak to Daddy. Roosevelt had gotten elected for a third term. Daddy had voted for him and Mama hadn't. Roosevelt was going to start something called "the draft." All young men would have to serve a year in the army. Mama was boiling mad.

When politics came into the conversation, I usually got away as fast as I could and tried to think about something more pleasant. On that particular day, I *had* something more pleasant to think about.

I thought I had finally figured out a way to get a puppy. If I could pull it off, it would be a miracle, so I tried not to get my hopes up.

Chapter 8.

MY DREAMS COULD COME TRUE

Every Wednesday we got the *Kansas City Star,* a Missouri newspaper from Kansas City. Regularly, I had watched the classified ads for a puppy. This time one jumped off the page at me. Puppies for sale in Beattie, Kansas. They were Shepherd and Collie mixed for $5.00 each. The ad said the mother was a good stock dog. I tried not to get overly excited. I had learned it was not wise to count on anything too much because I'd surely be disappointed.

I waited until suppertime to show my dad the ad. My brother Charley would be there. He had said he'd buy me a dog if Daddy didn't. Well, that was the last I had ever heard about it.

At supper, I had the newspaper folded up in my lap to the page where the ad was. When everyone had finished eating, I moved my plate

72

aside and prayed for the courage to appeal to my dad.

"You guys, I've found what I want for Christmas," I said.

"What are you talking about? Christmas is almost three months away," Mom said sharply.

I looked straight at my mother. "I'm not talking about next Christmas, Mom, I'm talking about last Christmas!"

Daddy gave Mom a quick look that said, "Don't say anymore."

I pulled the newspaper out and put it on the table in front of me. Very slowly, I read the ad to my dad.

"For Sale: Collie-Shepherd pups. 8 weeks. Mother, excellent stock dog. $5.00 each. Will crate and ship. A.J. Mullins, 650 Lester Street, Beattie, Kansas."

"I want one of these pups. I just need your permission to get one. I have the money."

"Where did you get money?" Daddy asked me.

"I earned it. I got paid $10.00 from Mrs. Sipes for tutoring Benjamin. I helped him with his reading for about six months until he caught up with the rest of us kids." I pulled the ten dollar bill out of my overalls pocket and placed it on the article.

"Where is Beattie, Kansas?" Daddy asked

Charley who drove trucks all over and would know.

"I think it's over by Manhattan someplace," he answered.

I had looked it up in our road atlas. "I know where it is. It's across the Missouri River and about another sixty or seventy miles. Nobody has to take me to get the puppy. I'll write the owner, send him the money and have him ship it on the train. I've checked with Mr. Million at the depot. He said the puppy would only be on the train for about two and a half hours."

Lucille offered to help me write the letter. That was nice. But Daddy still hadn't said I could do it.

Nobody said anything. I sat there waiting until I felt warm tears streaming down my face.

"Well, I guess you aren't gonna let me have the pup," I cried, getting up from the table. "Why did I ever think you would?"

Lucille and Irene stared at my dad.

"Now I didn't say she couldn't have it," he said to everybody else but me.

I had written the letter already. I pulled it out of my pocket and put it on top of the money. It was addressed and had a three cent stamp on it. I held it up for my dad to see.

"You'll have to pay freight charges. You can't

just send five dollars when you don't know how much the freight is," Mama said.

"Mr. Million said I didn't have to send them freight money. He told me to write in my letter that I'd pay the freight in Watson when the puppy comes in."

My brother laughed. "Looks like you've thought of everything. The only thing left to do is mail your letter."

"No, I need two fives for my ten," I said, wiping away the tears. My sisters were smiling. Maybe it was true. Maybe I was going to get my puppy. Maybe this was a dream. Hadn't I dreamed about this day?

Charley reached in his pocket to find two fives for my ten. Daddy offered me another ten. I nearly fell off my chair.

"If you must have a dog, I'll pay for it," he said.

"No. I don't want your money. I want this dog to be mine. I want something that I can call my own." I told him.

"The dog will be your dog," he smiled a rare smile, "no matter who pays for it."

The next morning, after my chores, I tore out of the house to mail my letter. Trudie at the post office said it would take about two days to get there. I knew the wait would be unbearable. I asked the owner to ship the pup as soon as possible. If he did, I could have it here in three or four days. Mr. Million promised to call me as soon as it arrived. I could tell he was happy for me.

He said, "You mean to tell me you are finally getting a stock dog?"

When I answered yes, he said, "Well it's about time, honey."

It was a cold Friday in October. I was so happy, I was walking on air. By Tuesday, I would have my dog.

Mr. Million was my friend. I saw him again that afternoon, like I did every day when I took our cream to ship to Omaha. I loaded the can on the drawbar of our tractor and drove it to the depot. Our cream can held five gallons. It was heavy. Hardly anybody could lift it, but I could lift it with one hand. In fact, I had to lift it up on the baggage table at the depot. The baggage table came up to my chest. Mr. Million had a hard time lifting the can with two hands. I did it easily with one.

One day a girl, the only snooty girl in town, came over to me at the depot as I was getting ready to unload the cream can. I asked her if she would put the can on the baggage table for me. I told her my back hurt.

"I can't lift that," she said.

"Try, please," I begged her.

As hard as she tried she couldn't move it an inch. Finally, showing off, I picked it up with one hand and put it on the table. She stared at me for a while and then walked away. When she looked back I was smiling at her.

Once in a while, if a kind gentleman were at the depot, he would offer to lift the can on the table for me. I'd say, "O.K., thank you," and then I'd watch him struggle with the heavy can. Mr. Million always got a kick out of that.

The next day, one of our sows had a new litter of pigs. I caught Daddy with a pine stick. He was about to knock a small runt pig in the head. He said it was going to die anyway and he didn't have time to fool with it. I couldn't stand it. I screamed and begged and pulled on his arm.

"Please don't kill it, Daddy. Give it to me. I'll take care of the poor little thing," I cried.

"You'll have to bottle feed it," he said. "It's going to die anyway. It can't live."

"I have to try," I told him, taking the pig out of his hands.

I put him under my coat and headed for the house. Mama said to put it in a box by the stove. I claimed the pig as mine. I was convinced that God had sent the pig to me to help take my mind off the puppy. It did help a little.

Every chore I had to do I did more quickly to get back to the pig. I even slept with it. Strangely enough, I was dreaming about my puppy and sleeping with a pig. The second morning, he actually ate like a pig. As the day progressed, so did little Timothy. That's what I named him. Although no one told me, I *thought* it was a boy.

Mama and Daddy went to the movies on Sunday afternoon to see *Citizen Kane* starring Orson Wells, but I stayed home with my pig. Next week I'd go with them to see the new *Dr. Jekyll and Mr. Hyde* movie, anyway.

Irene had gone out to Dr. Gray's pond to go ice skating with one of her boyfriends, Billy Gene Adams. He was tall and friendly.

Another of her boyfriends, Lowell Phillips, had gotten caught chewing tobacco in school. The principal had noticed the bulge in his cheek and stood talking to him long enough until all Lowell could do was swallow the stinking stuff. He just about puked up his socks.

One afternoon, when Lowell came to the house to see Irene, I was out shooting sparrows. He held a round metal lid out from his body and dared me to shoot it. What an insult! I could shoot a match off a fence post thirty feet away.

He was wearing a heavy coat. So, I pumped

the B-B gun just once and shot him in the belly, which of course was covered by that heavy coat, so it did no damage. The B-B of course, fell to the ground.

"You missed," he laughed.

"No she didn't," Irene told him. "She hits everything she aims at. She aimed at your belly." It was my turn to laugh.

With my parents at the movies and my sister gone skating, I had the house to myself and I loved it. I held Timothy on my lap and told him all about my puppy. I knew my dog would be the smartest and best stock dog in the whole state of Missouri, maybe in the world.

Tuesday came and no puppy. I kept bugging Mr. Million. He finally told me that when the puppy came, it would arrive on the late afternoon mail train coming from Kansas.

I began to worry. All kinds of things popped into my head. Did the owner get my letter? Was the owner a crook? Did he just keep my money? Did he really have puppies? Did something happen to mine? I didn't care if it was male or female. I just wanted a pup, more than I had ever wanted anything. I had told everybody about my dog. All the kids at school knew and inquired about it every day.

I got home just in time to see two young bo's

coming through the front gate. They were clean and friendly-looking guys, and they were hungry, like all the others. Mama had gone to get a permanent. Lucille and I were there alone. We both decided that these two were harmless. They had a half-grown yellow dog with them. They introduced themselves as Hoss and Critter. The dog's name was Wyoming. They were about the same age and height. Hoss was plump and nearly bald. Critter was slender. The dog belonged to him.

Hoss said the freight they had come in on would be in Watson for about an hour. They wanted to get back on it so they could get to Omaha where a friend had told them he had a job for them if they could get there today. But they did offer to help us with work.

Lucille told them they didn't have to work. She didn't want to be responsible for them missing out on a job. The job was for a wrecking yard that had a couple hundred old cars coming in. Their job would be to help tear down the vehicles, then record and store the parts. They were excited to have the work. Daddy would have liked these two young men. He took a liking to anyone who was willing to work hard and make an honest dollar.

Lucille filled two plates with food and brought

out a pitcher of milk and four big pieces of fudge. They ate quickly, thanked us properly, put the fudge in their pockets for later, and hurried to get back on the train. We wished them luck.

Little Timothy was doing great. He followed me all over the farm. I could see that Daddy was surprised at how strong he was, although he never said so. In a few days I would try giving him back to his mother.

All the grownups were talking about the war in Europe. Everyone was sure our country would get involved. The Germans were sinking our ships. Our American boys were dying. I tried not to think about it.

All I could think about was my puppy. I could only guess if it was a boy or a girl. Now, was not the time to select a name. After all, I'd be able to choose a more suitable name after I'd seen the dog.

When Thursday came and went without word from Mr. Million, I gave up hope. Why did I ever think it would happen? Maybe I just wasn't meant to have a puppy.

Chapter 9.

I LEARNED TO CRY FOR JOY

On Friday morning I woke up with a terrible headache. Mama said I was making myself sick, worrying about that dog.

I tried to keep busy. Not a difficult task on our farm.

The bo's came, but they were few and far between that winter. Just like the birds, they'd gone south to warmer weather. Warmer is better when you have to sleep outside at night.

About noon that day, Junior Barnhart ran his motorcycle into a sitting train on the tracks in Watson. The Ellisons lived by the tracks and they saw it happen. Iva said that the bike did a flip backwards with Junior on it and came to rest in a roadside ditch quite a ways back. He broke one finger and got a lot of bruises. He claimed he had fallen asleep while riding his favorite mode

82

of transportation.

Daddy went to a livestock auction in Rock Port. He gave me a list of things to do while he was gone. The biggest job was loading a wagon with hay from one of the big stacks. Then, it had to be run through the grinder and blown into one of our grain bins. I had to wear a scarf over my face to protect my lungs from the dry hay dust.

After the job was finished, I went to the house to get a drink of water. Mom had the radio on. I heard a man telling about a new invention that sounded great. It was called an aerosol can. He said it would be used for everything from paint to shaving cream.

Mama didn't get excited about it. She said that she and all her lady friends were waiting for someone to invent an automatic dish washer. Wouldn't that be something! But she thought that was really too much to hope for.

I heard more about television from our neighbor. He said that tobacco, cigarette, and soap companies were already preparing to advertise their products on "the tube," as they were calling it, in the form of paid commercials. To them it made good business sense. John Q. Public would be able to watch television without having to pay for it. More families would own television sets if they didn't have to pay to watch, but they would have to put up with commercials.

I could just see my mom having a fit when she saw a cigarette commercial on television. A pretty girl standing there smoking a Camel cigarette? That would really make her mad. But, there was probably nothing to worry about. I doubted if television would ever come to Watson. We listened to cigarette commercials on the radio. In fact, Daddy didn't want me to listen to Frank Sinatra's Saturday Night Hit Parade. Why? Because the show was sponsored by Lucky Strike cigarettes. They'd begin the program by saying, "Have you tried a Lucky, lately?" My parents didn't like that.

Daddy listened to the Grand Old Opry from Nashville and they advertised tobacco, but I guessed that was all right because it was *his* show.

In those days, there were only a few brands of cigarettes. I remember Camels, Lucky Strikes, Chesterfields, Phillip Morris and Kools.

Daddy came home late, after I had done all the chores. I hadn't seen the sun all day. That morning, when we had gone to the barn, it was ten degrees above zero. I warmed my hands by the lantern. I knew if I touched a cow's bag with cold hands, I might get kicked.

Later, when I took the cream to the depot,

Mr. Million looked at me with a sympathetic face and said, "Maybe today, Colene." I hoped he was right. I prayed he was right.

Mama made homemade potato soup and hot rolls for supper. What I managed to eat was delicious. Despite Mom's good cooking, I had no appetite. I had lost weight. No one had noticed.

After the supper dishes were cleared away, I sat down to do my homework. Usually, I had no homework, but lately I had not been able to concentrate at school. My friends had stopped asking me about my puppy. Some of them thought I'd lied.

It was pitch black outside by the time the evening mail train arrived. I heard it come to town and I heard it leave. My heart sank. I put on my coat and grabbed a flashlight to go out to our outdoor toilet. It was a cold trip. When I walked back through the back door, the phone rang. It was our ring. I ran to the phone as fast as I could, hoping.

"Hello," I said anxiously.

"Is that you, Colene?" It was Mr. Million.

I couldn't speak. Words would not come out of my mouth.

"There's a little boy dog here in a crate and he's whining for someone to come and get him," I heard him say.

"O.K." I managed to say, finding my voice. "I'm coming."

My heart was pounding, my ears were ringing, and I felt joy from my head to my toes!

Mom and Daddy guessed the puppy had arrived. I already had my coat on. I grabbed my gloves and the flashlight and ran the two and a half blocks to the depot. By the time I got there, Irene was behind me in the car. I hurried through the door.

There in front of me was the most beautiful, sweet ball of white I had ever seen. I fell to my knees by the crate. The puppy was wiggling and smiling. His mouth was wide open and his tongue was hanging out. He was as anxious to get to me as I was to get to him. Mr. Million pried the lid off the crate as quickly as possible. I couldn't wait to hold him. He stood on his hind legs and licked my hands. I hugged him and kissed him and hugged him some more. The puppy kissed back. I decided then and there that we were meant for each other. He was born to be mine, and he was all mine--nobody else's. I cried and cried. Never before had I been happy enough to cry, nor had I understood that kind of tears, until then. I didn't care who saw me.

I thanked Mr. Million. He had tears in his eyes and so did my sister. She hugged me and my puppy. This had to be the greatest moment of my life.

I didn't want to go home. If I'd had a secret hiding place to take my dog, just him and me, I would have run all the way.

Before long, the news was all over Watson. My puppy had come in on the evening mail train.

I was glad my family liked the pup. How could anyone not like him? Mama warmed some milk for him. He lapped it up quickly and, smiling, asked for more. I was surprised that Mom didn't care when he spilled a few drops on the kitchen floor. She said she'd take care of him for me when I was at school. She was being surprisingly understanding. I wanted to hug her, but she had never hugged me, so, I thought I'd better not.

Even Timothy liked my puppy. He licked the pig's face and the pig liked it. During the evening, I put him out several times to pee. He had to learn that Mama wouldn't like it if he peed on her clean floor.

That night I slept with a pig and a puppy in my bed. I got up in the night and put them both outside to go to the bathroom in the snow. When I woke up the next morning they were side by side. I was curled up around them.

Daddy took Timothy back to his mother. Sometimes, sows won't take their babies back.

Luckily, Timothy's took him back. Daddy said he heard the mother talking softly to her returned baby. When he left them, Timothy was nursing with his brothers and sisters.

Just to make sure all went well, I kept an eye on him. Daddy had given the pig to me. I still felt responsible and probably always would, no matter how big he got.

Then Daddy told me something that surprised the heck out of me. He said in about a year and a half, Timothy would be a mother herself. Nobody had told me that Timothy was a girl. Well, you learn something new every day. From that day on Timothy became Timothella.

The puppy didn't stay small for long. He was going to be a large dog just like I knew he would. I must have tried ten different names on him before he reacted to one. I let him choose. He had to have a special name. Not a usual dog's name, but one that fit him perfectly. I just knew the pup would let me know when I called him by a name he liked. I was pleased with the name he chose.

He became Nikki.

Nikki filled a vacancy in my heart. He listened to every word I said. No one ever had. Every job I did, he tried to help.

By the end of May, when school was out, he

was too big to carry. Nikki never let me out of his sight. He was smart. He learned commands quickly. Already he knew "come," "stay," "heel," and "fetch." When I went to get the cows, so did he. The first few weeks I carried him. After that he walked with me.

When he was about a year old he could go all by himself. At first, though, he was in training.

Lucille had gotten married in February and moved to St. Louis with her new husband. He was short and paid more attention to other girls than he did to my sister. She sure could pick `em.

We still went to the movies on Sunday afternoons. I got to see *Dr. Jekyll and Mr. Hyde, Dumbo, Sargent York* and *The Maltese Falcon*, starring Humphry Bogart. I didn't know what women saw in him. I thought he was quite homely.

One day after school, when some bo's were helping Daddy with the milking, I got to play baseball in our front yard. We always had a backup catcher, since we pitched toward the busy road in front of our house. This time, Betty Patton, my cousin, was batter. After she hit the ball, she slung her bat. I was the backup catcher. The catcher ducked, missing the bat. I didn't see it coming. The bat hit me square in the forehead, and it knocked me out cold.

Our neighbor boy, Randall Sharp, ran for home. Since he always got blamed for everything, he figured he was in trouble. But it wasn't his fault.

I guess my mother was screaming about getting me to Dr. Gray's office. Mama did not know how to drive. Randall's dad came running over to see if he could help. I always wondered why someone didn't run to the barn to get Daddy. And I don't know were our car was, but Mr. Sharp offered to drive me in one of Charley's trucks. All the kids piled in the back.

My forehead was swelling up into a round, red lump. I was still unconscious.

When I woke up in the doctor's office, I felt like I'd been "hit in the head by a baseball bat," for sure. Dr. Gray had given me a shot for pain, but it still hurt. His nurse, Carry Proppe, was holding an ice pack on my head. She asked me how I felt. I laughed. As much as I hurt, I laughed.

There were five or six kids who had jumped in back of the truck to get me to the doctor. Randall had run all the way there to see how I was doing. They were all standing around, gawking at me. When I laughed, they did, too.

"She's alive," someone said. But I didn't much

feel like it. I had to go home, lie down, and take it easy for a couple of days.

Nikki stayed by my side. When I complained, he whined.

Daddy called my dog to go with him to get the cows, but Nikki refused to go. I missed two days of school and two days of work. After that, I got back to work as usual, but the lump on my head and the headaches didn't go away for about two weeks.

The day we dug our potatoes, I did something stupid. Daddy had hitched two mules to our one-ton, two-wheel cart, and had driven them out to the center of the potato patch. He had already plowed the ground to expose potatoes of all sizes, which were lying everywhere. Iva, Laura, and Billy Ellison were there to help us. Daddy paid them a little money and a lot of potatoes. We each had a bucket. Once we had filled our bucket with potatoes, we'd go to the cart to toss them in. The mules just stood and patiently waited. After I had picked up several dozen buckets of potatoes and dumped them into the cart, I was getting tired. It was then I noticed that all the mules had to do was stand there. We did all the work. Without thinking, I picked up a clod of dirt and threw it at one of the mules. Naturally, it scared him. He jumped. When he did, all the potatoes went flying out of the cart. So, not only did I have to pick the potatoes up the first time, I had to pick them all up again.

Nashville Ned came again in the summer. In fact, he came several times that year and helped out with the haying and wheat harvest.

My brother, Charley and Fred Leisman, a man who worked for him, pulled the combine out of the machine shed where they had gotten it ready to cut our wheat. I wondered how Daddy had gotten my brother to do it. I saw them go to the wheat field, but for some reason they didn't stay out long. When they came in, I heard them talking about the roller not working. The roller turns around and bends the wheat back for cutting.

When the guys went into the house to get a snack, I took a look at the combine. I had to laugh when I saw what the problem was. Charley and Fred were both good with equipment, but they had missed the simplest thing. The roller was on backwards. Most likely, when they had taken it off to grease it, they had put it back on wrong. I got some tools and turned it around. It took about five minutes. Afterwards, I went inside to tease them about little sister having to fix their problem.

One Sunday afternoon, later that year, my dog

and I were sitting out in one of Charley's trucks, listening to the radio. President Roosevelt came on with a news flash. The Japanese had bombed Pearl Harber in Hawaii and wiped out a large part of our Navy. I ran to the house and told Mom to turn on the radio. When she heard the news, she began to cry.

"I told your dad that Roosevelt would get us into war," she said. "I wonder how many of us will have to send our sons off to die in some foreign country?"

I didn't know if Mr. Roosevelt was responsible or not, but what Mama said worried me. I had a feeling that this time she was right. Our young men *would* be going off to war.

Chapter 10.

1942 - THE WAR AND A CITY TEACHER

Japan's attack on Pearl Harbor brought the United States officially into World War II. As Mama had predicted, young American men, including ones we knew, began leaving to fight in Europe and the Pacific.

With the war going on, nothing was the same. News of the battles was on the front page of every newspaper and on every radio station. So many of our men were getting killed. Japan was beating us at every turn. They had been preparing for this for a long time. We had not. Daddy said, "Don't worry, we'll beat them yet," but we worried, just the same.

At home on the farm, something remarkable had happened. Nikki turned out to be the best stock dog anyone had ever seen. I was so proud of him. Not just because he saved me countless steps and enjoyed it so much, but because he was so loyal to me. No one had ever loved me like Nikki did. When the bo's or anyone outside our family came, he stood between me and them. Mama didn't have to worry about bums anymore, not with Nikki around. He wasn't vicious, just protective.

Every day when I came home from school, my dog was waiting for me at our front gate.

This year, I did not like my teacher, Mrs. Lewis. She didn't know anything about farming or farmers. Most of us kids lived on farms and we thought she looked down her nose at us. I couldn't imagine what she would say when she heard that my family fed hobos at the supper table. She'd think I was low class for sure.

Walkabout Tommy was still a mystery. He showed up several times a year and visited with my dad. Before he left, Daddy would hand him an envelope from the desk drawer. The only time he ever ate with us was one Sunday afternoon when we were making homemade ice cream. Twice I saw him eating in the cafe in Watson. Strange for a hobo.

Did he have something on my dad? Was my daddy having to pay him money to keep his mouth shut? I never heard of my dad doing anything illegal. I'd asked my sisters. They didn't know; if they did, they weren't telling.

Nashville Ned showed up in April with some bad news. Stove Pipe had passed away. It happened when they were working in the Florida orange groves. One day Stove Pipe didn't show up at noon at the lunch tables. Ned went to look for him. He found his friend leaning against a tree. He had sat down to rest and died there.

Mama cried. "We'll miss him, Ned. He was a good person."

There weren't many young men left in Watson. They'd all gone off to fight. Trudie, at the post office, said it was hard to keep up with the mail. Watson's servicemen were receiving lots of letters from family and friends at home. I wrote two or three letters a week to boys we knew, and included my funny poems and a stick of gum. The guys liked my poems.

That year we planted an even bigger garden and more potatoes. Daddy said we'd have to share with the families whose menfolk had gone off to war. Mama even bought more baby chicks, so there would be plenty of fried chicken and eggs. People said we were lucky that we had plenty to eat. Luck didn't have anything to do with it. We worked our tails off to have what went on our table.

Other countries had joined the United States in

the war effort. They were called "Allies." Still, we were losing the war. The Japanese had taken 76,000 of our men prisoner. They themselves would rather have died than be taken prisoner. Consequently, they had no respect for our men. One American commander surrendered his troops simply because they were starving to death. Once in the prison camps they continued to starve to death and were tortured and killed.

The government sent cases of khaki colored yarn to our school. We kids learned how to knit to make scarves for our soldiers fighting in cold countries. At first I wasn't very good at it, but the more I thought about a soldier lying in some bunker in the snow, the harder I tried to learn. Finally, I got so good at it that I could knit in my sleep.

Something unexpected happened in my classroom. Raymond Madron lived on a farm like me. He had missed three days of school that week. When he told our teacher he had to help his dad in the field, she didn't believe him. She called him a liar; she said parents didn't keep their children out of school to work. She flew into a rage, ran up to her desk and got a heavy wooden ruler. She told Raymond to spread his hands out on his desk. When she raised her arm to come down on his hand with that stick, Raymond grabbed her arm.

He looked squarely up into her face. "If you hit me with that stick for telling the truth, you won't be teaching school here no more,"

"What did you say?" she shouted.

Benny Collins came to his rescue. "Mrs. Lewis, if you hit him, you'll have to hit us all. We all have to stay home from school and help out when our dads need us to work our farms."

A couple of strong farm boys, Raymond's friends, got up and stood by his desk.

Mrs. Lewis sat down, but she was still angry. It took a while for things to calm down in our classroom. To top it all off, the next morning when Raymond's dad brought him to school, he gave the teacher a good tongue-lashing.

"My son doesn't lie and don't you ever accuse him of it again, Missy! When he says he's helping me, he is."

Mrs. Lewis was so upset, she dismissed school for the day. We all hoped that meant she would not be back. The school board excused our class for the rest of the week. The following Monday, when we returned to school, we met Mrs. Luttrell. She had retired from a school in Rock Port, but had been hired to finish out the year. She was a great teacher.

In July, my brother Charley was drafted into

the army. It was hard on our family. We wondered if we'd ever see him again. He was sent to Fort Leanardwood in Leavensworth, Missouri for his basic training. We placed a star in our front window. It meant we had a family member in the military service.

Fewer and fewer hobos showed up. They, too, were helping out with the war effort and had found good jobs in "War Plants," as we called them, or factories that made anything from bullets to bombers. Now and then we got a letter from one of them.

In August, Mickey Manduco showed up on a very hot day. He had a boy with him. I was now nearly thirteen and he looked to be about fourteen. I wondered what a kid was doing riding the freights.

The boy's name was Robert. He didn't ask for anything, but Mama brought out a pitcher of lemonade from the ice box and we sat and talked for a while.

"Do either one of you want to work for a few days? My husband could sure use some more help. With all the young men gone off to war, it's hard to get day workers," Mama said.

The bo's looked at each other. Mickey was never short of money. He entertained on the streets and on the stage. He just had a need to travel and see the country.

"We don't need the work or food, just wanted to stop by and say hello. You folks have always been so kind to all of us when we needed help, though. We'll be glad to help out for a few days," Mickey told my mother. "Is that all right with you, Robert?" he asked.

Robert kind of scrunched up his face. I thought he was nice-looking even with his face scrunched up.

"I don't know anything about farming," he laughed, "but, yes, I'll be glad to help if someone will show me what to do."

"Are you a city boy?" I teased.

"Yes, are you a county girl?" he teased right back.

"Well, it's too hot to do much of anything today. My husband has gone out to the river to buy some catfish for supper. You are welcome to eat with us."

"Catfish?" Robert asked. "I don't think I've ever eaten cat-fish. Where I come from, we eat shrimp and lobster and clams. I can live on fried clams."

"I've never eaten that kind of fish. Where are you from?" I asked.

"Massachusetts," he answered. "And for a while I worked in New York."

"You are awfully young to have a job," my mother said to him.

"Well, if you want to eat you have to work." he answered.

Mama asked the same question that everybody asked. "Don't you have a family, son?"

"No ma'am. Just me." he said.

My mother looked concerned, but she asked nothing else.

A gentle breeze had come up, making the afternoon a bit more bearable. Mickey had gone to sleep under the shade tree.

Mama and I had to wash fruit jars--hundreds of them. They had been put away clean, but had to be rinsed and sterilized again.

That night we'd pick more tomatoes. Early the next morning, regardless of what the temperature was, we'd begin the hot job of canning. We still had the wood cook stove on one side of our big kitchen, but now we had a gas cooking stove on the other. We'd fill the quart fruit jars with cut tomatoes and put them in canning kettles to boil on the stove. Because of the heat, the job would begin at four a.m. By six o'clock, the fire in the wood stove had to be out or it would be us that cooked. The sun came up early. Only the gas stove was used after that. I'd have to stop canning to do the milking and then I'd be right back helping my mother.

Robert pitched in and helped to clean the jars. He was friendly, but fairly quiet.

After a while, I got up the nerve to ask him about his family. What he told me was the saddest thing I had ever heard. I didn't always like my family, but at least I had one.

Chapter 11.

ROBERT'S STORY - A NEW FRIEND

"We lived in Lowell, Massachusetts. My father worked as a lathe operator for the Boston-Maine railroad. I had a good mother and two younger sisters. Georgia was eight and Gloria was ten." I was beginning to wonder. Robert said he "had" a father and mother and sisters.

"Last Christmas," he continued, "we had our house all decorated with lights outside and a tree inside. Somehow, in the night, the tree caught on fire and burned our house down. I had a bedroom over the garage, so I was the only one who got out alive. It all happened so fast."

"I am so sorry Robert. Maybe I shouldn't have asked. Don't you have relatives? Grandparents, aunts, uncles or somebody you could live with?"

"No. My dad was an orphan. My mother's family disowned her when she married my dad.

They were Catholic. My dad was a Baptist. There's no one."

"What did you do?" I asked.

"I took a job setting pins in a bowling alley and rented a room up above it for pretty cheap. The money wasn't bad, but I got so lonesome.

"Then one day I took a train down to Boston. There was Mickey out in front of the Old North Church where Paul Revere hung his lantern, entertaining the tourists. I stayed behind after the crowd left to catch their tour bus. He asked me if I knew a good place to get some lunch. I took him to my favorite place to eat fried clams.

"We struck up a friendship. Come to find out, he was on his own, too. He taught me how to juggle and do some magic tricks. So while he's entertaining people with his music and singing, I entertain the kids. It works out O.K."

While Robert told me these things, he never looked up from his work. I probably shouldn't have asked, but I'm glad he told me. I think he had wanted to tell me, although I had a feeling that he didn't talk about it much.

Robert and Mickey continued cleaning jars, while Mama got supper and bottled the milk for delivery.

Daddy was back in time to help with the milking. It was hot as the devil in the milk barn.

We hurried to get it over quickly.

Once in a while I got a whiff of Mama's catfish all the way out from the kitchen. She'd cooked a whole platter-full and stuck it in the oven to finish it up in her special way.

There were lots of "war widows," as we called them, living in Watson, just as there were in every area of the country. Their husbands weren't dead, at least not all of them; they were away fighting the war. The "war widows" didn't have a lot to live on. Every now and then, one of them would tell my dad that they couldn't afford as much milk anymore, so they'd have to buy less. My dad would always say all right. Sometimes they'd tell him to bring one quart instead of two. However, we continued to take the same amount. We just never charged them for it. They would protest, but Daddy didn't care. He kept on taking it. He also took them food from the garden and once in a while potatoes, eggs, and fresh meat or anything else that we had to spare. On holidays, everybody got fresh cream for whipping, free.

Mama's catfish supper was a success. Besides the fish, there were American-fried potatoes, tons of fresh vegetables from the garden, cornbread and store-bought ice cream. It was rare to *buy* ice cream. We always made our own, but the day had been too busy.

Robert said the catfish was almost as good as fried clams.

After supper we picked several bushels of tomatoes and stored them down in the cellar where it was cool.

Daddy set up cots under the walnut tree for he bo's. They loved it. It was still too hot to sleep. I told Mama I was going for a walk around Watson. Robert asked if he could come along. I looked at Daddy to see if it would be all right. He had no objection.

I had never been able to talk to boys. With Robert it was easy. I was beginning to wish he lived nearby so we could be friends and see each other often.

Watson's main street was about two and a half blocks long. The stores were all on one side of the street. On the other side was a city park and just beyond that the railroad tracks and the depot. I showed him where I brought the can of cream and told him about getting my puppy. Nikki had come along on the walk, as always. At first, my dog didn't take kindly to Robert. But Robert liked Nikki and after a while, they became friends.

We walked by the high school and the grade school. We walked by the Baptist church where my family attended, he Methodist church that the Ellisons attended, and by the Presbyterian church.

My sister, Irene, had been asking Mama if she could visit the Presbyterian church. She said they had a new, young preacher that was really handsome. Mama said no.

Once, while Robert and I were walking along, our hands touched. We were both embarrassed and moved apart. For a few minutes, neither of us spoke. When we did, we both spoke at the same time. Then we laughed and cleared the air.

Town was quiet. Nothing was open for business except for Charley Christian's gas station. Robert bought us a Cherry Mash candy bar. He had quite a bit of money. I figured that juggling paid pretty good.

I *loved* Cherry Mash candy bars. Every kid I knew did, too. They were shaped like a mound. Delicious chocolate and crushed peanuts on the outside and pink cherry flavored filling on the inside.

Robert and I talked about movies like *Casablanca* with Humphry Bogart and Ingrid Bergman. I didn't know why she would make a picture with him. Then there was *Road to Morocco*, with Bing Crosby and Bob Hope. That would be good. I hadn't seen it yet. Robert said he wanted to see *Yankee Doodle Dandy,* a musical with James Cagney. I wanted to see *Bambi,* even if it was a kid's movie. Then we talked about how Clark Gable's wife, Carole Lumbard, had recently been killed in a plane crash.

I couldn't believe I was talking to a boy! This boy said he wished he was old enough to enlist and help out with the war.

Why would anyone want to go to war? I wondered.

"As soon as I'm old enough and if this war lasts long enough, I'm going to enlist in the first branch of service that will take me," he said as a matter-of-fact.

"I hope we'll win this war soon. I want my brother to come home," I said.

"Your brother? I noticed there was a star hanging in your window," he said.

"My older brother, Charley. He's in Fort Leanardwood and about to be shipped overseas someplace."

We enjoyed our walk so much that for the next couple of evenings we took walks. One evening we walked all the way around our farm. It was almost three, and one-half miles. We picked violets by the railroad tracks and gave them to Mama.

My sisters teased me about Robert. But I

didn't care.

Robert and Mickey stayed on for three days to help us catch up. Mickey had a show booked in New Orleans, so they had to leave. They didn't ride the freight this time. They had money for tickets. I hated to see them go, and that was a first for me. Usually I couldn't wait to get rid of a boy, but Robert was different. I walked to the depot with them and told them good-bye. Robert shook my hand and held it for a moment.

"I know I will miss you," he said.

I felt my face turn red, but quickly answered, "Me too."

I watched the train until it was completely out of sight. I wondered if I'd ever see him again.

Chapter 12.

A Chicken Story and a Flat Tire

In January we heard on the news that 60,000 Americans had been killed in the war.

Recovering from the attack on Pearl Harbor had taken time, effort, and money. Every American was dedicated to winning the war. Just as Daddy predicted, we were finally showing the Germans and the Japs what this country could do. Now we were winning some battles and as Daddy said, "Kicking their behinds."

In February we beat the Japs on a scrap of land located at the southern tip of the Soloman Islands in the Pacific called Guadalcanal. The natives in that area risked their lives to bring American pilots, forced down behind enemy lines, to the safety of American bases.

Then we stopped Rommel, one of Hitler's top generals, in North Africa. In March our U.S.

bombers prevailed in the Bismarck Sea. But, all these battles cost American lives. So many deaths.

The war cost money--lots of money. We attended war bond rallies to help raise that money to pay for the costs of weapons. We wanted our fighting men to have everything necessary to get the job done. Even at school, we kids took a quarter at a time and bought government stamps. When we got enough saved, we could trade them in for a bond. The bonds we purchased were backed by the government. It was their way of saying, give us your money now to help win the war and we will give it back with interest when the fighting is all over. U.S. war bonds sold for $18.00. In ten years we could cash them in for $25.00. We had faith in our country and knew we would win the war. All Americans were supporting our service men and women.

People who had never planted gardens were doing it now to help produce some of their own food. They were called "Victory Gardens." There were shortages of all kinds. We were told to "Use it up, wear it out, make it do, or do without." Nobody ever had to tell my family. We had always done that.

Coffee and flour were rationed then. You couldn't buy a new car or new tires. Everybody's tires had so many patches, they looked like they'd had black chicken pox.

I worried about Robert. I wished he'd write. I had never asked him to, but I hoped he would.

Lucille's husband was drafted into the army from St. Louis. I never thought they'd take the little twerp. They had a boy named Harry Richard, after his two grandfathers. Lucille would move back to Watson until the war was over.

Lucille and Harry lived with us for a while. Harry loved the farm animals. We hauled him all over the farm on the tractor and in the wagons, so he could get to know the place. As soon as he could walk, he began chasing chickens. We had chickens of all ages. At night they went in to the chicken house to roost, but in the day they were free to run all over the farm.

I graduated from the eighth grade. Irene graduated from high school. It was no big deal to me. I figured we still had four more years to go. I wasn't planning on any celebration until I was off the farm and on my way to college.

When I was mowing our tall alfalfa that summer, I accidently cut a half-grown chicken's leg off, right at the knee. I didn't see it until I noticed it on the ground behind the cutting bar, flopping around.

I stopped to see if I could help. The poor thing didn't appear to be in pain. Strangely enough, it wasn't even bleeding, just scared. I felt so sorry for the it. I knew it couldn't walk like that. We would either have to eat it or make it a peg leg.

I found a short stick in the tool box and some black electrical tape. I held the stick next to the chicken's leg to make sure it was as long as the other leg. I wrapped it good with the tape. When I put the chicken down it hopped away on that peg as if it had been that way all its life. I had to laugh. As the chicken grew, I'd catch him and make him a longer leg.

Later, when the chicken grew to full size, Daddy had a cement man come and put down a sidewalk from our house to the well. Naturally, "Peg Leg Pete" walked over the fresh cement and left his strange marks. Daddy saw him do it. The cement man was going to go smooth it out. Daddy told the him to just leave it. Daddy scratched something by the tracks. It said, "Peg Leg Pete- 1943." That chicken was pure pet and died of old age on the farm.

Everyone found going to the movies to be an escape from the war. My favorite new movie was *Oklahoma*. It had great songs like, "Oh What a Beautiful Morning" and "The Surrey with the Fringe on Top."

That darned Walkabout Tommy continued to show up. My dad still met him with an envelope. Would I ever know what that was?

Charley wrote to us as often as he could. He was with the Army Engineers in Europe. They built pontoon bridges to get our troops across the water and then blew them up so the enemy couldn't use them. A pontoon bridge was a bridge built out of wood on top of metal barrels-- all scrap material. They fulfilled their purpose.

Although the hobos weren't afraid of work, they found it difficult sticking with an indoor job for any length of time. I guessed they were so used to being on the go, it was hard to break the habit. Occasionally, one would show up and tell us where he'd been working.

Appalachia Man, California Carl, and River Johnny had been by at different times. They would work for a while, quit the job, travel around a few days, and then go find another job. There was plenty of work in aircraft factories, ship building, ammo plants, tank and gun makers, etc.

Daddy cut his hand clear to the bone on our 30" buzz saw. We were cutting up logs for fuel. A log slipped, pushing his hand into the blade. Doctor Gray sewed it up and told him to keep it clean and that meant not doing any farm work.

So, guess who got to do it all? But school was out
and I was used to it.

While I was discing a sixty acre parcel with the
M Farmall, one of the huge back tires went flat.
I knew with Daddy being laid up, I couldn't ask
him to help me. I walked back to the implement
shed and backed out the smaller tractor. Then I
loaded the heavy-duty jack onto the drawbar.
With a mall and some tire tools I managed to get
the tire off the hub. Getting it up on the back of
the other tractor wasn't so easy. Daddy had
taught me how to make leverage work for me,
using a steel pole instead of my back. That was
good information when you're a 110 pound kid.

I tied the tire on the back of the tractor and
took off for Rock Port, fourteen miles away,
seven of them on the highway.

The men in the tire shop couldn't believe I got
that tire off by myself. It hadn't been easy. I
could do just about anything when I had to. It
had taken about an hour and a half. I hoped
Mom hadn't missed the sound of the tractor in
the field. She'd have had a fit, had she known I'd
driven to Rock Port on the tractor.

By the time I got the tire back on, it was time
to get the cows in and do the milking. I wasn't
about to tell Daddy what I had done. No use to
worry him. Somebody had to do it. Who else was

there? Just me.

The following Sunday we went to my Aunt Hattie's and Uncle John's in Rock Port for dinner. Uncle John asked me right in front of Mom and Daddy what I'd been doing in Rock Port on the tractor. Mom darned near died when she found out. Daddy just looked at me.

"I don't know how you did that," he said.

"To tell you the truth, I don't know how I did it, either."

When Charley left for the war, he was engaged to a girl in Rock Port. It would be a long engagement. Irene was also engaged to a high school boyfriend. He was in the Army Infantry.

With gas rationed, no one could get far from home. We did a lot of socializing with our neighbors. At our house we played carom on a square, wooden game board with pockets. We played a card game called muggins, my dad's favorite. In the evenings, we listened to programs on the radio and ate a lot of popcorn and fudge made with saccharin, a substitute sugar. With sugar rationed, we were left with this horrible tasting replacement. I can still remember how bad it tasted. However, our sacrifice was small compared to what our fighting men were having to endure.

We wondered if the war would ever end.

Chapter 13.

WRITING, BEATINGS, AND SUGAR

I knew from the time I was young that I was good at telling stories. By the time I was eight, I had written lots of stories and poems, and I never stopped. When we were given a writing assignment at school, I loved it. My friends liked my stories. When it was an assignment, they'd tell the teacher, "Read Colene's story first." My teachers encouraged me to continue with my writing.

What was so hard for some of my classmates was easy for me. Of course, they all had talents that I didn't. I hated sports. My friend Iva was good at them. My sister Lucille was a great cook. Not me! Irene was good at making friends. I kept more to myself.

I wrote about real people and fictional characters. I kept a daily journal about my life

117

on the farm and at school. Although my daily routine stayed pretty much the same, there was plenty to write about on the farm--from the wonder of a new calf being born to a robin pulling a worm out of the ground to feed her babies. I wrote poems about planting crops and stories about the harvest. I even wrote stories about the shapes of the clouds in the sky and fantasized about the mysteries beyond them.

Although I was always writing a story in my mind, I had little free time to put them on paper, except in the winter when Daddy wasn't in the fields. Then I'd keep my room toasty warm with the wood stove and Nikki and I would stay there for as long as Daddy didn't need us. I would write and he would sleep.

I can't remember when I realized I would be a writer. I'd always known it. That's the one thing I loved to do.

I hoped to win a scholarship for college. My grades were good, so my chances were excellent. I sometimes had nightmares about being stuck on our farm forever.

I was the youngest in the family and soon I would be the only kid left at home. Glenn was married, Charley was in the army and had never done anything on the farm when he *had* been home, Lucille was married, and Irene would be next to leave. Then it would be me, Mom, Daddy, and all that work left behind.

Daddy had been complaining about some gypsies parked outside of town and hidden in the trees. When the gypsies were around, things came up missing. The gypsies were thieves. Daddy was explaining the problem to a hobo who had been invited in for supper.

"You want to get rid of those gypsies? I'll take care of it for you. Hobos hate gypsies. They give folks on the road a bad name with their thieving ways. Hopper John came in on the freight with me. I'll find him this evening. We'll scare them thieving varmints off." He laughed a mischievous laugh.

Hopper John dressed like a railroad engineer. He wore striped overalls and cap, a blue shirt, and had a red handkerchief tied around his neck. He said dressed like that, he could go anyplace he wanted to in a railroad yard. Smart, I thought.

By morning the gypsies were gone. Hopper John knew a lot about these roving bands of people. He said they believed in such things as witches, magic, and casting spells upon anyone towards whom they thought unkindly.

On the way to the gypsy camp, Hopper John collected some dry bark off a sycamore tree and three bird feathers.

The sun had just come up when they arrived. No one was in sight except for an old woman sitting on the step of a travel wagon. The others were out stealing breakfast, no doubt. In sight of the woman, Hopper John made a palm sized mound of dirt on the ground and slowly placed the feathers in a triangle around it. He topped off the mound with the sycamore bark. Quickly, he mumbled a few meaningless words and put a match to the dry bark. As the bark blazed he threw both hands in the air and turned with his friend to leave. As the old gypsy woman looked on, she was sure he had put a curse on their camp.

With a silly grin on his face, he whispered, "Well, that ought to do it." The hobos had had some fun. Daddy thanked them for their help.

The telling of the event made me the most popular kid in school that day.

When so many of our teachers went off to war, a great many of the older ones came out of retirement to help out.

We got Miss Birdie Besinger. She dressed funny. On a comfortable day she wore fur because she was in her eighties and cold-blooded. She was nearly blind. The kids were always showing off in her class, doing things to tease her, but she was a good teacher and we all liked her.

She kept a little black book on us. Three marks by our name and she punished us. If your shuffled your feet, you were in trouble. One day in study hall, three of the guys--Donald, Junior, and Dwayne--got to teasing her. They took her little black book and tossed it around to each other. Junior was standing by an upstairs open window. Without thinking, sure enough he threw the book out the window. It was all a joke and Miss Besinger was enjoying the fun.

Immediately, Junior ran downstairs and outside to get the book. He brought it back and handed to her and told her they thought they had teased her enough for one day.

Our principal, Mr. Mitchell, heard about it. Miss Besinger had gotten a kick out of it, but Mr. Mitchell was mad. He took the boys down to the science room for punishment. We could hear him yelling from all the way up in study hall. Miss Besinger was afraid of him.

The two middle fingers were missing from Donald's left hand, from an accident, since he was two years old. That's the hand Mr. Mitchell chose to beat on. He took a board from the back of an oak chair, had Donald put his hand on the desk, and beat it until it looked like raw meat.

Junior got the same across his back. Dwayne took off out the front door to go tell his dad.

As soon as Mr. Mitchell left the room, the suffering boys fled the building and ran to the doctor's office about two blocks away. Dr. Gray called the sheriff and he called the boys' parents. He also called all the school board for an emergency meeting at the school house that night. The entire town turned out.

Mr. Mitchell got fired. Two weeks later, his wife found him dead in his barn. They said he died of pneumonia. But the truth of the matter was that someone had beat him to death. The casket was not opened at the funeral. His wife didn't say much, since her husband would have gone to prison anyway, and she thought she might be next. Mama said Mrs. Mitchell was afraid of the parents in Watson. As I recall, Watson people did look out for each other.

When all that was over, I turned my thoughts to a problem I had at home. Something maybe Charley could help me with.

Charley was Mama's favorite child. If he didn't like the food on the table, she'd get up and cook him something else. She never did that for any of the rest of us. Getting older and smarter, I tucked that information away for later use. Charley could get Mom to do anything.

Knowing that, I planned to write him a letter and ask for his help. I needed a horse now to help bring in the cows. We'd never had a saddle horse to ride. The large Belgium horses we owned were bred to pull heavy loads and farm machinery.

Daddy had opened up pastures on the far side of the railroad tracks for the dairy cows. That meant the cows had to be brought back and forth across the tracks four times a day. Even with Nikki working one side of them and me the other, when we crossed the tracks, sometimes the cows would run down them. I hated it. Not only was it dangerous, the cows could outrun me. By the time I got them in, I was worn out, so I wrote to brother and told him how bad I needed a saddle horse to bring them in. I also told him that I had $75.00 to pay for one. In those days you could buy a great saddle horse for $75.00.

Timothella, the runt pig that I had raised, grew up quickly, like pigs do, and had a litter of twelve babies of her own. I reminded Daddy when he sold her and her babies that those pigs were mine. It was I who saved her from the club and death and it was I who fed and watered the hogs twice a day. So I told him flat out, for the first time in my life, that the money was mine. I was surprised that I had nerve enough to say so.

I was more surprised when he wrote me a check for $75.00. I opened up my own bank account and saved it.

I'd begged for a horse just like I begged for my dog. I never asked for anything I didn't need. My Nikki had been a lifesaver. I wish I could have taught him to milk cows.

When I wrote to Charley, I told him why I needed a horse. I was the only help that Daddy had and he knew it. Even though my brother never did do much on the farm, he was aware of the fact that I did the work of two men. I didn't know if he would write back to Mom and Daddy for me or not, but I had to try.

It worked. About a month later the letter came. But Mama didn't like it. This time, not even her favorite child could convince her.

"You'll get yourself killed on a horse," Mama said."You're not going to get one and that's that."

For some reason, my dad didn't pay any attention to her.

"Now Mom," Daddy said, "that boy is over there fighting for his country. If he thinks we should get the girl a horse to help with the work, then I think we ought to do it."

Was I hearing things? I kept my mouth shut like I usually did, and prayed.

"I'll call Scammons," he said. "Once in a while he sells horses at the auction. If we're gonna get you one, we'll get a good, well- trained one."

Mama didn't like it a bit, but Daddy had made up his mind. In a few days we drove over to Scammon's ranch. I was shown several decent horses, of all colors and kinds. I had never been on a horse, but I had worked behind horses and mules all my life.

I liked what I heard about a gorgeous, five-year-old sorrel mare. Mr. Scammon's daughters had numerous ribbons and trophies with her. The daughters were now married and gone and had no interest in her anymore.

I wanted to ride her. She was a spirited horse and if I'd had any sense I'd have been afraid of her. But I wasn't. Mr. Scammon told me she was a five-gaited horse. He saddled up his own gray stallion and rode along beside me, showing me how to get her to trot and single-foot. The rest was easy. The horse was smart and wanted to please me. I had an idea she truly was a girl's horse. I didn't care about all the fancy footwork, but I was happy to know she had even won ribbons for herding cattle.

I definitely did not want an old, used up, plug of a horse.

"I want this one," I told my dad. "She's got

spunk."

"That one costs the most money," Daddy said.

"How much?" I asked.

"Seventy-five dollars," Mr. Scammon answered. That was a lot of money for a horse. He must have known how much money I had.

"I'll take her," I said, dismounting. I reached into my pocket and came out with my own checkbook.

My dad asked, "Are you determined to pay for this horse yourself?"

"Absolutely," I said.

The first thing I did when we got her unloaded at home was get in the saddle. I wanted to ride her all the way around our farm. Little did I know that the horse had never been near the railroad tracks. We were about a half-mile from the house when the train whistle let out a blast. The pony stopped, reared up on her hind legs, and almost threw me off. I held on tight. Then she took off running towards the house. The next thing I knew she was racing toward the machine shed and through the wide door. If I hadn't ducked, she would have taken my head off.

Mom saw it all. She came out yelling and screaming.

"You get off of that horse right now. You and your dad are taking it back where you got it. Do you hear me? Get off! You're going to get killed on that thing!"

Her yelling didn't help me calm the horse any. The poor thing was just frightened of the train. To please my mother, I got off and led her to the water tank to drink. I never said a word to my mom, but I wasn't about to return that horse.

After she drank, I removed the saddle, led her to a small pasture, and turned her loose. Nikki and I hurried away to bring in the cows. I had no intention of listening to my mother yell and scream.

I knew that the pony would get used to the trains after a few days. I thanked God that my dad felt like I did. The pony *would* settle down. Daddy told Mom to be patient and give it some time.

Every couple of hours I would go to the fence and pet my horse. I watched her when the trains went through. At first she ran the entire perimeter of the pasture, kicking up her heels. But she always came to me when I went to the fence. On the third day, I went into the pasture and played with her. She loved being combed and brushed.

On the fifth day, when no one was around, I saddled her up without incident. She stood with the saddle on until after the 10:30 passenger train had passed. Then I mounted and road her all over the farm. She was wonderful. I could hear the passenger train pulling out of the station. She paid no attention to the whistle.

I told Daddy to be out of the house with Mom after supper. I wanted her to see how smart my horse was and how gentle. At first Mama would not look. The Lincoln Zephyr (train) was blowing its whistle. When she did look, she could see that the pony was no longer afraid of trains. No matter what, my mother never did approve of me having a horse. But from that day on, between my horse and my dog, getting the cows across the track was quite simple.

I named my horse "Sugar." I named her Sugar, because she made my life a lot sweeter.

After Mama got to liking her, she named her "Stockings." I thought that was a ridiculous name and anyway, it was *my* horse. Sugar had four white legs, from her hooves to her knees. That was where "Stockings" came from. I thanked God no one ever called my horse "Stockings" but Mama.

Chapter 14.

ROBERT COMES AND LEAVES

Daddy said the war was coming to a close, but a lot more men were going to die before our enemies were defeated. Sixteen million Americans were in uniform.

On the farm, life went on. I didn't have time for much of a social life. The only places I went were the Sunday afternoon movies and out-of-town basketball games. I hated playing basketball. There were no other sports available to me in our small high school. Everyone had to suit up. I thought we looked silly out there on the court in shorts and makeup. Some of the girls liked it, but I thought we looked like a bunch of clowns. My body was capable--I had the ability to run and jump--but my heart was never in the game. And I was shy. My worst fear was that I'd hit a girl too hard. Unlike the boys, we played half-court. Maybe I should have played on the boys team.

Everybody that played got a letter. So, at the end of my freshman year, I got a letter. Big deal, a white felt "W" to sew on a sweater! I was proud of Watson and I was proud of our high school, but that "W" meant no more to me than the game ever had. I threw it in a box. There would be three more years of high school and three more letters to go.

The Ellison girls were still my best friends, but they had other girlfriends besides me. I didn't. Boys liked me, but I was never all that interested. None of them compared to Robert.

When Mom, Billy Ellison, and I were out putting in more garden one morning, guess who showed up. It was Mickey Manduco and Robert. I hadn't been aware of a train coming in.

Mama didn't get another lick of work out of me for a while. I was so happy to see Robert, I almost cried. I thought I would never see him again.

Mickey and Mama sat under the walnut tree and visited. Robert and I sat in the front porch swing and talked about everything. He looked more grown up and seemed to have put the sadness of his family's death somewhat behind him.

He and Mickey had been somewhere in Nebraska. Mickey's sister had passed away and they had attended her funeral. Robert said that since they were so near, he wanted to come and see me. He told me he had thought about me every day since he'd been gone. I was glad because I had thought about him, too. He told me how much he'd enjoyed our long walks around Watson.

They were heading for an aircraft plant in St. Louis. Mickey intended to retire his accordion until after the war.

Mickey told us, "It looks like I am going to have to help get this war over with."

Robert was too young to get a job there.

"What will you do?" I asked him.

"Don't worry about me. There's plenty of work. I can always get a job. I want to work and save for college, but in December, I'll be old enough to enlist. College will have to wait."

"What do you want to go to college for?" I was curious.

"You may think I'm crazy, but I have plans. I hate it when I see a small business go under because of their poor business skills. I want to learn everything there is to know about running a business so I can help. I want to take businesses that are failing and train management and employees to do a better job. Teach them how to make money," he laughed. "But first I have to learn how to do it."

No, I didn't think Robert was crazy and I told him so. I thought he was smart and ambitious. Somehow I knew he would be successful at anything he chose to do.

Robert helped Mom and me plant the garden. He had never planted anything in his life. He couldn't believe how tiny the seeds were.

Daddy let them sleep in Charley's bedroom. He wasn't using it.

After supper, Walkabout Tommy showed up again. He and Daddy sat in the living room and visited for a long time. The man was curious about Robert.

Daddy and I were up early the next morning, doing the milking while everyone else was asleep, even Mom.

Daddy told me he had something important to tell me. He said Tommy'd had a chance to talk to Robert quite a bit the night before and had learned about the boy not having a family.

He asked me to help him keep a secret. He told me Tommy was wealthy and a kind-hearted man. He'd just gotten sick and tired of big business in Texas. After his wife died, he decided to turn the company over to his grown children.

"Tommy's sister sends money to our post office box. He knows he can trust me. When he shows up, I give him the money."

So that's what it was. Now I knew. My dad was not a crook, after all.

Daddy told me that Tommy had taken an interest in Robert. "He wants to take him to Texas to his ranch and give him a home. He'll send the boy to college and see that he gets off to a good start."

"Oh Daddy, that's wonderful! But Texas? We'll never see him if he lives that far away," I said sadly.

"But just think what an opportunity that boy will have," Daddy said.

"Does Robert know yet?" I asked.

"Robert knows. He's thinking it over. It came as quite a surprise to him." Daddy told me. "Tommy asked if I'd keep Robert here for a few days, to let him decide."

"Did you say yes?" I hoped he had.

"Of course. You'd like that wouldn't you?" he smiled that rare smile.

I was happy and sad all at the same time. Robert would be given an opportunity to go to college. That's what he wanted.

The last time Robert had been with us, I'd wanted him as my friend. But this time I liked him in a different way. I felt more attracted to him. I could tell that he liked me, too.

Mickey Manduco left Watson the following afternoon for St. Louis. Tommy must have spent the night in town somewhere.

Robert helped with all the work that day. He was not an experienced milker, but he tried. We set out cabbage plants and more onion sets. Everything had to be watered. We pumped buckets full of water and carried them to the garden from the well.

"You and your family put in 12 to 16 hour days. Do you always work this hard?" Robert asked.

"Yes, sometimes harder. Winters are worst. It's what we do and it's what I've always done, but not what I'll do forever. I'll never marry a farmer! I am a writer. I intend to get an education and live in the city," I told him. Robert wasn't the only one who had dreams.

Each evening, Robert and I went for long walks or sat in the porch swing and talked. When the moon came up the last night he was there, we sat close together in the swing and held hands. I wished our time together would never end.

I cried myself to sleep, knowing that he would soon be gone and our time together would be over. He was that one special friend that I had never had.

Walkabout Tommy showed up with train tickets for the both of them. Robert didn't know for sure where in Texas they were going. Daddy knew. Later, I'd ask him.

This time I asked Robert to write to me and he said he would. Before he left, not knowing what to say, we just stood there for a few minutes, looking at each other and holding hands.

As soon as they left for the depot, I went out and rode Sugar for a long time. Work could wait. I didn't want my family to see me cry.

Irene went to Colorado Springs in June to marry her boyfriend, Gene, who was in the army. She stayed there with him at Camp Carson until he was shipped overseas. I felt so sorry for her when she came back to Watson to wait for his return from the war. In November he was wounded, but not bad enough to be sent home.

Robert wrote as he'd promised he would. He turned seventeen in August and in December he enlisted in the Coast Guard. That was the only branch of service that would take him at his age. His new guardian, Thomas James, signed papers so he could go.

After he enlisted, I never heard from him

again. I missed him so much and prayed that he would make it back alive.

Chapter 15.

MICE, MULES, AND SNAKES

My sophomore year of high school came to an end. Hard work in school had resulted in good grades. I knew if college was in my future, funding would have to come from me. My older brothers and sisters had not expressed an interest in going on to school, but I wanted a good education. If I continued working, a couple of scholarships would be mine at graduation. That would help. Daddy told me he hadn't paid for college for the other kids in our family, so he wasn't paying for me. I pointed out to him that my brothers and sisters didn't want to go to college. I did. But it made no difference.

I had no intention of milking cows and farming all my life. I had vowed I would never marry a farmer. I had nothing against farmers. No one knew better than I how hard farmers work to

137

feed the world.

When the war began, farmers were encouraged to produce as much food and grain as possible to help the war effort. We raised corn and wheat. Much of the corn we fed to the stock, simply because we made more money selling milk and cream than we did selling the corn. We sold any corn that was left over. The wheat was a good cash crop.

My dad and I were pushed to the limits to produce as much as we could. I thanked God for Sundays. On that day, we only did the chores. When I had to leave early for a game, Iva and Laura helped me with the milking so that I could get there on time.

One thing I never did was let anyone see me dressed in my work clothes, unless they happened to be on our place while I was working--even when I was younger and wore overalls. My hair was long but always clean and curled. I wore bright, feminine blouses my mother had made. Mom made sure I at least *looked* like a girl.

That was one thing I admired about my mother. Although she came from a poor family, she knew how to dress. She was very pretty. She sewed clothes for herself and for us girls. Mama always wanted her girls to look good, so when I was particular about my clothes, she was glad to help me.

With both my sisters gone, the farm was one lonesome place. The work kept me busy, but I was determined to have some kind of a social life. Several boys had asked me for dates--boys that I had known all my life. Once in a while I'd go to the movies or out for a hamburger or something with one of them. They were like brothers my age that I had never had. Glenn and Charley were so much older.

Every Friday night there were square dances at our high school. Mom and Daddy never went, but I did, once in a while. They were lots of fun. Everybody danced with everybody. Even when corn-harvesting time came and I'd come in from the field bone-tired, I still attended the dances.

We finally got electricity and more tractor-pulled farm equipment. Life was somewhat easier. But one thing never changed: we milked the cows by hand, twice a day--rain, snow, or sunshine.

In April, our American soldiers had gotten a solemn lesson in what they were fighting for, when they helped free the survivors of the Nazi death camps. Lifeless, decayed bodies were stacked like corn wood outside the gas chambers. The survivors were too weak to turn the pages of a book. Our guys offered them food and watched them share every morsel. I saw a picture of a negro soldier as he watched and wept.

Finally, on May 7, 1945, Germany surrendered. One down and yet the Japanese to go. Japan was beaten, but they refused to surrender.

U.S. planes dropped leaflets on Hiroshima. They read, "Your city will be obliterated unless your government surrenders." Next, Japan was ravaged by bombs, but still no surrender. Our government was desperately trying to put an end to the war.

One day that summer, Daddy and I were heading toward the barn with an overflowing wagonload of freshly mown hay. Nothing in the world smells as sweet and fresh as new mown hay, especially if it's alfalfa. City folks drove through the country in the evenings at haying time, just to get a whiff of it. We should have charged them for the priveledge. The haywagon was being pulled by Doc and Dolly, our team of horses. Daddy was up front, driving them. I was on top of the load in the middle of the wagon, lying flat on my back, enjoying the rest and the blue sky. We had crossed the railroad tracks without any trouble. Nikki was running along behind, through the hayfield, which was always full of mice. Once in a while we'd even throw one up with a pitchfork-full of loose hay.

Suddenly, the worst thing that could happen, happened. A frightened field mouse crawled up the leg of my blue jeans. I stood up, hoping to shake him out. The terrified mouse hung on to my leg.

Daddy was looking straight ahead, so, right there on top of that load of hay, I took off my jeans to get rid of the mouse. Out it ran, scurrying quickly across the hay and out of sight.

Problem was, the section men--the men who repaired sections of the railroad tracks--were headed down the tracks toward Watson on their quiet, motorized flat car. There I was with my jeans off and my hind side up in the air, flashing my pink underwear in the sunshine.

"Hello Colene!" someone shouted to me.

It was Bob Gaines, a boy I went to school with. He worked for the railroad and was on that car.

I turned around and sat down in the hay. It was too late. All the men were waving at me. I was so embarrassed; I could have cried.

Bob Gaines must have told everybody in Watson. The next time I saw Iva, she said she heard the section men had all seen me with my behind stuck up in the air. One way or the other, I knew I'd eventually get even with Bob Gaines.

That summer I could not stay out of harm's way. Every time I turned around, I was injuring myself. One time, I ran a pitchfork through my leg. Well, not all the way through, but nearly to the bone. It hurt something awful! It was actually caused by a snake. I hated snakes. Especially rattlesnakes. They scared me to death!

One was curled up in the shade of the barn when I went to put the feed in for the cows. I heard the rattle and tried to get around him. He came after me. I ran to the barn and picked up a pitchfork. I meant to stick him with it, but my foot slipped on a board that a cow had peed on, making me ram the pitchfork into my leg. I hollered and scared the snake. He turned and went the other way.

I found the peroxide and bandages in the first aid kit in the shed. By the time the milking was done, the hole in my leg felt like the Grand Canyon. It had swelled up and hurt like the dickens. Mama told me to put some ice on it and that would help with the swelling. I tied a rag around my leg to hold the ice in place so I could finish my chores.

The ice helped the swelling, but the pain continued.

After that experience, I hated snakes even more, especially rattlers. If I could have found that sucker, he'd be dead.

I was foolish enough to keep a date that night. Dwayne and I went to the movies. When we arrived, the theater was full. We had to stand up through a double feature, a dumb thing to do with a sore leg! I would never be stupid enough to do that again.

The next day it was back to work. Dad and I used our team of mules when we picked the corn. As we picked the ears off the stocks, we threw them into a wagon. If we used the tractor, one of us had to get up on the tractor and drive it farther down the row every few minutes. It was a pain. However, if we used the team, all we had to do was tell them "get up!" to pull up a ways and "whoa!" to stop.

We'd had a full day of picking corn. Afterwards, we still had the chores to do. Later that evening, Daddy asked me if I'd go out to the barn and put some salve on a sore spot on the hind leg of our mule, Jack. The mules were tied to the manger where they were eating hay. There was a distance of about eight feet behind them to the wall. On the wall were wooden pegs where we hung their harnesses.

Instead of speaking to the mule, like you're supposed to, I walked up behind Jack and touched his leg with the salve. It startled him so much, he kicked backwards with both hind feet and got me directly in the chest.

I flew into the wall and all of the harnesses came down on top of me. I sat there for a while, wondering if I could get free from the heavy leather mass and make it to my feet. I was thankful I had not been kicked in the head. The blow would have killed me.

I staggered to the house to find my parents. Dad had gone to deliver milk. My mother was coming in from gathering eggs.

"Mom, I think you'd better get me to the doctor. I feel like I've got something broken."

"What!" she asked. "Where?"

I tried to explain, but everything went black and I remembered no more. The next thing I knew, I was lying on our couch and Dr. Gray was examining me and trying to wake me up. He was killing me, poking around to see if anything was broken. I hurt so bad that I thought my time was up. I expected the angels to come and get me.

The doctor gave me a shot to stop the pain. It was a while before it began to take effect. He didn't know what had happened to me until I told him I'd been kicked by a mule.

In those days, doctors made house calls. My mother must have telephoned him when I passed out.

When Daddy came home, he and Mom took me to the Hamburg Hospital for ex-rays. I had some broken ribs. I had to stay in the hospital overnight. The next day my chest turned black and blue and stayed that way for a long time. I was miserable for weeks. In the hospital they taped me up so tight I could hardly move. But the tape helped--when I did move, I wasn't in quite so much pain.

I felt as sorry for Daddy as I did for myself. Every time Dr. Gray saw my dad, he gave him the devil for working me so hard. Plus that, Daddy had to hire a man for a few days to do my work. The fellow only stayed for two days. The work was too hard for one man, he said. Perhaps Dr. Gray was right after all.

After all this, I then made an addition to my plans for the future. I'd live in a snake free city that had more than one theater. But first, some- how, I had to make it off the farm.

On August 6th, one of our B-29 bombers had been ordered to drop an atomic bomb on Japan as a desperate measure. More bombs were dropped before the final surrender in September.

It was over. So much loss of human life, so many families torn apart--men would return without arms, some without legs. Some would be unrecognizable. The country would never be the same.

For us on the farm, life went on.

In September, my junior year of high school began. Lucky for me, I had Evelyn DeVore for my English teacher. She encouraged me to continue with my writing. I became editor of our school newspaper and loved it. I had found my niche.

Chapter 16.

1945-VICTORY-HELP AT CHRISTMAS

Irene's husband was discharged in November. He looked much older. Irene, Gene, and I went to Kansas City on the train to meet Charley when he came back from overseas.

The train depot was crowded with servicemen in uniform. It was hard to tell one person from another. At least Charley was coming back in one piece. Just like I knew it would be at the depot, there were men in wheelchairs--some of them with one arm, no arms, one leg, no legs, all of them so sad to watch. However, the war was over and we had won.

America was celebrating. There were shouts of joy all over the train station. People were hugging and kissing and crying when they located each other.

Irene spotted Charley first and started to

wave. We began making our way through the crowd toward him. Charley cried. He hugged Irene and Gene, looked squarely at me, and didn't know who I was. I had grown up while he was gone.

It wasn't until I said, "Charley, don't you know me?" that he realized who I was. I had changed from a young girl to a young woman.

Gene carried Charley's duffle bag as we made our way toward the exit door. Charley stopped here and there as army buddies would motion for him to meet their families.

We had a few hours to kill before the train left for Watson. We went to a movie and saw *Mrs. Miniver*. Then we ate and went to the circus. Since we were with a serviceman, we all got in free. Everyone was welcoming the men home.

Our train was supposed to stop in Watson to let us off. It was about two o'clock in the morning. Everybody from town was at the depot to welcome my brother. They all came out for every man and woman who returned.

Problem was, the engineer forgot to stop. He kept right on going. Charley got up and told the conductor.

The conductor patted my brother on the shoulder and said, "Don't worry son, we'll get you home."

A few minutes later the train stopped and backed up to Watson's depot. Everybody had gone home. Charley took off running the two and a half blocks to our house.

When the hugs and tears were over, Lucille got on the phone and told Mrs. Bowers to spread the word, "He's home."

It was the middle of the night. Watson got dressed again and hurried over to our house. Mama had prepared tons of food.

Watson had street dances and celebrated for weeks.

The only sad thing about Charley's return was that after he got off the ship, before boarding the train for Kansas City, he'd called his former girl friend, the one he'd been engaged to. She had written to him all along, but had never had the heart to tell him she'd gotten married. He didn't act too hurt, just surprised.

So, our family was one of the lucky ones. Our men had lived through it. Some families weren't so fortunate. But what about Robert? Why hadn't he written? Was he all right? Maybe I would never know. Maybe I was not meant to know. Still, I cared.

Lucille divorced her husband. He'd written home and said he had met someone else. That was way back when he was in basic training.

Didn't take *him* long. She went to work and her son, Harry, stayed with Dad and Mom and me quite a lot. We loved him. We nicknamed him "Gabby," because he talked before he could walk, and never stopped talking.

Lucille and Harry had their own little house in Watson. Irene and Gene lived in Watson, too. I was glad that my sisters were near.

Every so often, once the war was over and jobs were scarce again, a hobo would show up. One evening, a fellow knocked on the door, looking for work and food. This one had come in on an extra evening freight train. He called himself "Movin' Man." Daddy handed him a plate of food out under the walnut tree. He sat there for a while and began reciting poetry, all to himself, one poem after the other.

Lucille and Irene had come over for supper. Following supper, as we used to do, we headed for the piano. Irene played hymns and the three of us sang.

Movin' Man began to sing with us. My dad, recognizing a well-trained baritone voice, did something he had never done before. He invited the fellow in to the living room to sing with us. Movin' Man sang so well that we just kept quiet and listened. He told us that he had sung professionally for many years. As he left by the front gate, he was still singing. We never knew what talents a hobo would bring with him.

The railroad had cracked down on the bo's riding the freights. They had to be careful or they'd land in jail. I felt sad, knowing those days were just about gone forever. Most of the hobos who could work re-established themselves with good jobs during the war and were able then to re-establish their lives. At least some good came out of the war.

Jobs were few. The servicemen were given a small monthly check and could go to school on the G.I. Bill. Charley went back to trucking and to finding new girlfriends.

When the Christmas season rolled around, Daddy was laid up sick. I got to do all the chores, but I was used to it. This time, though, he was sick for quite a while.

It started snowing hard two days before Christmas. Sometimes I could hardly see the barn or the cows. On the day before Christmas, something wonderful happened that I will never forget.

I was walking out the back door of our house, bundled up like an Eskimo and loaded down with milk buckets, when, through the falling snow, I noticed that several cars were parked in our driveway. Men began piling out. They were all local war veterans.

Dr. Gray had made a few calls. He said, "Mr. Moore gave all he could give to your families while you were away. He is sick in bed and now he needs you. Go and help that daughter of his." And so they came.

"Put us to work, Colene," one of them said.

"Be glad to," I answered.

When the cows were all in the barn, it didn't take long to get the milking done. They were all farm boys. They knew how to milk cows. I didn't even get to help. They told me to sit down on a milk bucket. So I did. There was a lot of happy chatter in the barn that morning. Suddenly, we heard someone singing outside.

Our windmill was about fifty feet from the front door of the milk barn. The singing was coming from there.

Carly Hartman had come back minus a leg. Somehow he had managed to climb the slick windmill ladder all the way to the top. He was sitting on the small, wooden walk-a-round and, in his beautiful baritone voice, was singing "Joy to the World."

All the guys had to get to their feet and take a look. By the time Carly finished the carol, we all had tears in our eyes and were not ashamed.

Then someone hollered up to him. "Atta boy

Carly!" We all applauded.

The vets kept coming back morning and evening until Daddy was able to help out again. Not only did I enjoy the help, I enjoyed the company. They came Christmas day, too. It was a time I have never forgotten.

Chapter 17.

MURDER, THIEVES, AND A FARM SALE

I asked my dad if he could find out about Robert. Since he'd gone off to war, there had been no word. I wanted to know. Did he make it back? Was he all right?

Daddy had the name and address of the family Robert had gone to live with in Texas. They would know.

Mama told me it was not proper for girls to go chasing after boys and to forget about it. I would have to catch Daddy alone and ask him again.

I tried. Oh, how I tried. But I could never get him out of my mind, or my heart. I felt foolish. We were just kids. Maybe it was a case of "puppy love." But it sure was real to this puppy.

One night our neighbor boy and I double-dated with another couple. We went to Tarkio to a double feature. They turned out to be two terrible movies.

It was a cold February night. There were ice spots on the road, so we drove carefully. As we came around a dangerous curve between Tarkio and Rock Port, we came upon a bad wreck. Several cars were parked along the road. We saw an ambulance, one badly damaged car, a cattle truck and the local sheriff's cruiser.

The sheriff came over to our car and told us not to get out. He didn't want us kids to see this. Apparently, a preacher had hit ice on the curve and his car had slid under the truck. The man's body parts were being picked up off the road. We all got sick and headed straight for home, driving with painful care. It was difficult to stop thinking about someone having to pick up bloody body parts. I even had nightmares about it.

On Monday at school everybody wanted to hear about the wreck. Gwendolyn wanted all the gory details. I felt ill just thinking about it and finally went home early with a headache.

I will never forget Gwendolyn. She had been dirty since the first time I saw her in second grade. She had one clean spot in the middle of her face where she had washed her eyes, nose and mouth, simply because the teachers made her do it. Dirt was caked on her forehead and in front of her ears. Her clothes never were washed. In a word, she was *pathetic.*

Mom begged me to bring her home with me to spend the night. I did not want to, believe me. Mom told me she'd been wanting to get her hands on that girl and clean her up for as long as she could remember. Finally, I agreed.

After supper, without being too obvious, Mom took charge. Gwendolyn and I both had baths before we went to bed. Mom washed and curled Gwendolyn's hair, gave her a clean nightgown, and sent us to bed. Mom took her clothes, washed them, and dried them behind the heating stove. Early the next morning, she ironed them.

When we arrived at school that day, nobody knew who she was. She was actually pretty. All day long the kids told her how good she looked. From that time on she came to school clean, thanks to my mother.

Mom's two bachelor brothers, my uncles, George and Arley Patton, came to visit us for a couple of days in June. They did my work and I went fishing with about seven or eight kids from Watson. We fished for catfish from the bank and from under the Missouri River bridge. It was always so easy to catch fish the way we did. We used any kind of strong stick, some heavy string, bobby pins for fishhooks, and worms we obtained by kicking at the ground.

While we were fishing and trying to be quiet, yet have a good time, a fishing boat passed by. We heard two men arguing loudly. Right before our eyes we watched one man beat another man to death with a cedar stick. After he finished the job, he looked directly at us. We were all scared half to death. The man knew every one of us and we knew him. We stopped fishing immediately, got in the car, and headed home to tell our folks. Of course, our folks took us to the sheriff's office to report what we'd seen.

Luckily, the murderer got there ahead of us and turned himself in. He knew we'd all witnessed what he'd done. The sheriff took statements from each of us, but we did not have to appear in court. We thanked God it ended there.

A few months later, the man hanged himself in prison.

One morning, around the first of September, Nikki wanted me to go into the cornfield behind the barn with him. I thought it quite odd. He led me to a spot near the road that was out of sight of anyone going by. The corn was ripe and the stocks were tall. A lot taller than I was. My smart little friend wanted to show me a pile of corn that had been picked and piled up. Daddy and I hadn't done it. I wondered who had.

When I told my dad, he just grinned. He was almost sure that he knew who had been stealing corn from everybody. The thief picked it and piled it up one night and would come back in a truck to get it the next.

Daddy laughed about it. He told me not to worry and not to tell anyone, he'd take care of it. I didn't worry, but I sure was curious.

Daddy sat in the field that night, hidden, with a double-barreled shotgun and a flashlight. Along about midnight a truck pulled off the road by the pile of corn. Daddy had been right. They were two boys from town--brothers.

He sat and watched them load the corn on their truck. When they had it all loaded and were getting into the truck, he came out of hiding and pointed the flashlight and shotgun at them. I wish I'd been there.

He said, "That was really nice of you boys to come and load my corn up for me. Now take it on down to the elevator and leave it on the scales. I'll go down there and pick up my check for it in the morning."

Sure enough, the boys hauled the corn to the elevator. Daddy collected his money after the chores were done. My dad never told on those boys. But that was the last time anyone in our area lost corn.

In November my Dad had a slight heart attack, quite unexpectedly. The doctor said it was a clear warning. There could be others. This time he had been lucky.

My dad took it to heart, so to speak. He and Mom went to Rock Port and bought a nice house where they would retire.

It all happened so fast, I didn't know how to think about it. I was a senior and would graduate in May.

In January (1947) we had a farm sale. All the farm equipment and all of our livestock were sold at auction. Mom's chickens and equipment were sold. A lot of our furniture and household items were sold. Even my saddle horse, who had faithfully served me, sold for $575.00, $500.00 more than what I had paid for her. And it was all mine. I breathed a sigh of relief. School money. Yes.

Everything sold for premium prices. During the war, farm equipment had not been manufactured. Our neighbors flocked to buy. Everything we had was in good repair. Daddy and I had kept it that way.

One of our neighbors had just had a sale. Daddy said all their farm equipment was held together with bailing wire instead of being properly repaired. Everything sold for about half of what ours sold for.

I followed some men out to where our cows were about to be sold. I heard one of them say to another, "You'll have to pay a lot of money if you want one of these dairy cows. They are the best I've ever seen."

I felt proud that I had been a part of it. As hard as the work had been, I was sad to let go. I knew I'd miss the crowing roosters, the arrival of newborn calves, the smell of freshly plowed soil, and the sweet aroma of alfalfa. I'd miss open fields and the trains--especially, I'd miss the trains. How would the engineers ever get along without the farm girl on the gate? So, with mixed emotions, the door closed on that part of my life.

I knew that Mom and Daddy would be better off without the responsibility of the farm. Come fall, I'd be gone. What would they do without me?

All the family helped us move into the lovely new house in town.

On weeknights, until about the middle of April, I stayed in Watson with some friends. From then on, until I graduated, I drove back and forth from Rock Port.

Charley married a girl from Watson in the early part of May.

On graduation day, May 17, 1947, I was

miserable and frightened. Every day of my life, until now, had been laid out for me. From now on it would be up to me. I was determined to follow my dream. I asked myself if I could do it.

Again, I thought of Robert.

Chapter 18.

DREAMS FULFILLED

The house Daddy and Mom bought in Rock Port was wonderful. It had electricity and plumbing, so there was no more carrying in of wood and water. It was a good thing, because I wouldn't be there much longer to do it for them. There was no more going outside to the bathroom either. With plenty of electricity, plumbing, and a furnace in the basement, they were all set.

Mama was quick to take advantage of a sprawling garden area in the back.

I did get those scholarships--several in fact. I worked that summer after graduation in Rock Port as a cashier in a market. In the fall I attended a junior college not far from home. Two years later I went on to Columbia to study journalism. I knew what I wanted and I knew how to get it. Hard work! That, I understood.

Actually, the term "wanting to be a writer" didn't fit me. I'd been a writer all my life. Now I was determined to be better.

Nikki moved with us to Rock Port. He wasn't all that happy. Although there was a big back yard for him to romp in, there were no cows to herd and I was seldom home to play with him.

Alice, a lonely little girl in the neighborhood fell in love with Nikki. She was an only child. She came often to ask if she could play with Nikki or take him for a long walk. I was so grateful to her. Actually, she reminded me of me when I was her age. When I came home, I always brought her a present.

Arriving at home, Nikki would met me at the door and never leave my side. He still was my one true love. My heart ached every time I had to leave him behind. Some day, I would be able to take him with me.

My first job as a journalist was with a daily newspaper in Des Moines, Iowa. It was suitable for a first job, but still in too much of a farm community for me. Too many reminders.

After a year and a half with the paper, I was offered a position with "Exploring Business," an exceptional magazine, modern and entertaining. The magazine was located in St. Louis, across the state from Mom and Dad, but still in

Missouri. I could visit often and also see my sisters, who were excited about my new career.

I was hired because I was single and willing to go anywhere to do interviews with successful businessmen and women. The work was exciting. I was never in one place for any length of time.

A few men friends had come and gone. Perhaps I was overly particular. No matter where the assignment took me or how interesting it was, I couldn't get that young hobo out of my head. Actually, I wasn't sure I wanted to.

I flew to India to do a story on a man and his wife who bought and sold precious stones, for many years. They were delightful, intelligent people. And, very rich.

After India I visited a successful country and western artist who was born in poverty and rose to fame in concerts, movies, and records. He was also very rich.

I visited four foreign countries, one after the other. Although no two stories were the same, there was nearly always an area of sameness. Each story began with a dream, but it was ambition and hard work that brought success to the individual.

I had agreed to travel anyplace in the world on assignment, but when I learned my next stop would be in Houston, Texas, I was relieved. A successful businessman with a supposedly questionable background had granted the magazine an interview. I had never visited the Lone Star State, so I was looking forward to it. A camera crew was scheduled to meet me there on a preassigned day. Our hotel was grand, but still country. We listened to music by Eddie Arnold and Hank Snow on jukeboxes and on the radio.

Houston was large and full of friendly Texans. We dined at a western steak house called "Cowboy's Carousel." The lot of us were made welcome. We soon were aware that we were the only ones not wearing boots and western hats. It was made more obvious than ever that we looked different when the waiter asked, "Where ya'll from?"

The steaks were fabulous. Almost as good as my mother's. After our meal we tried our feet at dancing what they called "The Western Swing." Everybody was willing to teach us. We had a great time.

The next morning, the camera crew went on ahead of me to a towering office building where our subject, our "Mr. Successful Businessman," was located.

I arrived just before ten and checked in on the first floor. I was escorted to the top floor, the penthouse office, where the interview was to take place.

All I knew about this fellow was his name, R.W. Copeland. My appointment with him was scheduled to begin at ten. There would be ample time to catch our plane at three and be back to St. Louis by six p.m.

At ten, a friendly but businesslike receptionist told me that Mr. Copeland was ready for me. I collected my things and followed her into a gorgeous, spacious office. Large windows overlooked the city of Houston.

My interviewee looked to be the young man seated behind an elegant mahogany desk. He was jotting something down in a small notebook.

No one else was in the room except for the camera crew who had arrived earlier and was ready to film the interview.

I waited for our subject to look up before extending my hand to introduce myself.

After a moment, he rose from his chair and smiled a friendly greeting. "R.W." was one handsome Texan. He came around the desk to take my extended hand. He was attractively dressed and wore sharp black, western boots. He stared at me with a strange expression. Suddenly and quite unexpectedly, I realized who he was. I caught my breath and held on to the chair beside me.

"Robert?" I heard myself asking. Of course it was--a grown up version of the boy I'd never forgotten.

"Are you who I think you are?" he asked, smiling broadly and squeezing my hands. "Are you a country girl?"

He had asked me that the first day we met on the farm. The day he'd showed up with Micky Manduco.

"Are you a city boy?" I managed a smile. "You are R.W. Copeland? Why Copeland? And why did you stop writing to me? I've worried about you since we were kids." Thoughts of the interview went out of my head.

"I'm sorry." he said. "When I joined the Coast Guard during the war, I didn't know if I'd make it back or not. I didn't want to burden you with that. Then, when I did make it back, I still had no education. I thought perhaps your family might not be happy about you hanging out with someone who was practically a hobo. You have no idea how much I wanted to see you. I wondered if you had married someone. I hoped you hadn't. Now look at you! You are just as I remembered and you're still writing."

"I remember the night before you left for Texas. We were two kids sitting in the porch swing and holding hands," I said.

"I will never forget it," he smiled.

"You said you were going to make businesses better. Is that what you do?" I asked.

"Is this part of the interview?" he laughed.

The camera crew was waiting for instructions to begin. I heard one of them say, "I didn't know she knew this guy."

"Come on, let's get this interview over with. I want to show you Texas," he said. "I owe it to you. You showed me Watson, remember?"

"But Robert, your family," I said.

"I'm not married, are you?" he asked, at the same time turning my hand over to look for a wedding ring.

When I answered no, he grinned at me and said, "Then you and I are going to see Texas. It will take a while longer than Watson."

During the interview, the two of us caught up on each others' lives. Walkabout Tommy was really Thomas James, a man who owned a size-able chunk of Texas.

The hobos who befriended Robert when he was on the road told him never to tell anyone his last name, so he didn't--not even us.

After the war, he had studied business at a Texas university. After graduation, he repaid Thomas James, who was experiencing some postwar business losses. Robert had a knack for making money and a good education to back it up.

All the time I was interviewing Robert, he never let go of my hand. We were so happy to see each other after so many years. It was as if we had stepped back in time to when we were kids.

I thought about the day I'd gone to the train depot to pick up my puppy. I was so happy, I cried. I never felt that kind of feeling again until this day. Finding Robert had truly brought me joy.

I missed that three o'clock flight back to St. Louis. Three days later I returned to my office, filed the interview, and headed back to Texas. Never again would Robert and I be separated. We made sure of that.

Robert and I were married on his ranch, north of Houston. It was a beautiful, simple ceremony. Lucille and Irene attended.

The first thing we did was head for Rock Port to see Mom and Dad and pick up Nikki, who was no longer a young dog.

Robert's company, Lonestar Package, con-continued to grow and expand. My typewriter, my dog, and I accompanied him when he traveled to other cities on business.

We loved California and would always remain in Los Angeles for longer periods of time than necessary. Finally, after the death of Thomas James, we moved there.

Soon after moving to Los Angeles, our blond-haired, blue-eyed baby daughter was born.

A few years later, tiring of traffic, crime, and smog, we resettled in the lush, green Williamette Valley of Oregon, where the streams were clear and the air was pure. There were also plenty of theaters and no rattlesnakes!

My Robert took a liking to hogs, can you imagine? A business man like Robert? A city boy like Robert? And can you imagine me, back on a farm and loving it?

It all started when he bought a few cute pigs at an auction. The pigs grew up and had babies.

The pig population flourished and so did my writing. It's amazing how many stories there are in a hog barn! A lovely little runt pig named Priscilla was the first to inspire me to write about her and her kind.

I told my favorite hobo he could have all the pigs he wanted, but no cows. If he wanted milk, he could buy it at the supermarket.

Robert and I lived happily ever after, but I never forgot the things I'd grown up with--the things which had made me what I was and which would always be a part of me: the old farm, the hard work, the sweet smell of alfalfa, the homemake pickles and homegrown tomatoes, the war, the trains, and especially, the hobos.